All's
Forgotten
Now

MICHAEL S. RIPLEY

authorHOUSE®

AuthorHouse™
1663 Liberty Drive
Bloomington, IN 47403
www.authorhouse.com
Phone: 1 (800) 839-8640

Published by AuthorHouse 09/23/2019

ISBN: 978-1-7283-2817-1 (sc)
ISBN: 978-1-7283-2815-7 (hc)
ISBN: 978-1-7283-2816-4 (e)

Library of Congress Control Number: 2019914637

Print information available on the last page.

Dedicated to my parents (may they rest in peace), who instilled a love of reading in me from a young age; my friends who didn't laugh at me when I told them I was going to write a novel; and Jonell (because of everything).

Each night, when I go to sleep, I die. And the next morning, when I wake up, I am reborn.

—Mahatma Gandhi

Some pirates achieved immortality by great deeds of cruelty or derring-do. Some achieved immortality by amassing great wealth. But the captain had long ago decided that he would, on the whole, prefer to achieve immortality by not dying.

—Terry Pratchett
The Color of Magic

That is not dead which can eternal lie,
And with strange aeons even death may die.

—H. P. Lovecraft
Call of Cthulhu

CONTENTS

CHAPTER 1

Lost Souls

Detective Stephen Ramos took one last drag from his cigarette and then threw the glowing butt into the gutter, where it sizzled and went dark. He pulled his long wool overcoat closer against the damp valley fog, loathing the late night hour. He was supposed to have had the night off.

With his daughter, Maria, at a friend's for a Halloween sleepover, he'd finally managed an evening alone with his estranged wife, hoping they could save their failing marriage. He'd switched shifts with two other homicide detectives so his night off wouldn't be interrupted and taken Claire on an old-fashioned date to a fancy steak house in the rejuvenated downtown. Things had progressed slowly at first as they talked and tried to reconnect. He wanted her to remember why they'd fallen in love in the first place.

He knew his job was the primary issue that had driven them apart. For years she'd endured the costs of his being a homicide detective: his excessive time at work—both the early mornings and late nights—and the constant fear that he might not come home at all.

It wasn't until nearly two hours into their date, when they were sharing after-dinner drinks and dessert, that she'd smiled like she used to. For a brief moment, he felt hope for them. Then his phone buzzed, and he'd seen it was work. He answered. The dispatcher apologized, explaining there had been four murders so far tonight, and no one was left to cover. As he listened, Claire had gathered her things and left.

The clattering whine of an early-morning BART train passing a few blocks away brought him back to the here and now. Two police cruisers were already parked near the alley's entrance, their flashing red and blue lights giving the scene a deceptively carnival-like air. Across the street, in front of a rundown strip club called the Dancing Hut, several bleary-eyed barflies stood gawking at the spectacle while a pair of uniformed officers questioned them. Flickering above them was a garish neon sign with the silhouette of a woman sliding up and down a pole.

Ramos walked over and surveyed the scene down the trash-strewn alley. A man from Forensics used a flashlight as he picked carefully through the debris, looking for evidence. At the end of the alley, a security light cast a pallid pool of illumination around a battered dumpster. A camera's flash brought the scene into stark relief and revealed the city's chief coroner, Dr. Jerome Martin.

Ramos ducked under the yellow police tape and moved carefully down the alley until he reached Martin, who was scribbling in his notebook, his attire spotless and gray hair meticulously groomed. "So what brings you out to join us mere peasants so early in the morning, Dr. Martin?"

The coroner glanced up, registered the newest arrival with no expression, and returned to his notebook. "Good morning, Detective Ramos. While your attempt at jovial sarcasm is noted—and dismissed— my presence is due to several vacationing members of my department."

Ramos cleared his throat. "So what do we have?"

Martin stood up and pointlessly smoothed his plastic smock. He tilted his head toward the dumpster and with his voice flat, said, "The victim is a Caucasian female in her late twenties. Given her temperature, I'd say she's been dead for no more than three hours. She was bound and killed in another location. She suffered severe lacerations and bruising to her wrists and ankles, indicating a substantial amount of struggle on her part. The injury to the back of her head is most likely the cause of death."

Ramos hesitated and then forced himself to step over and look at the victim. He swallowed heavily and felt his stomach twist.

She lay on her side, naked and pale among the garbage bags. Even in death, her lean, athletic figure was extraordinary. She wore her raven-black hair in a practical bob. Her handsome, angular face was unmarred except for three drops of blood on her cheek. Her pale-blue eyes were half-opened, her exotic features frozen in a forlorn, weary expression.

Martin's voice intruded. "Despite her superior physical condition, nothing I've found sheds any light on her identity. She could be a ballerina with a professional dance company or a stay-at-home mom who loved to work out."

Ramos nodded silently and sighed. The mass of half-congealed gore on the back of her head marred the picture of physical perfection. He thought he could make out skull fragments and bits of brain tissue in the bloody mass.

He'd drunk too much wine at dinner and his head felt full of cotton. He needed another cigarette. He muttered more to himself than Martin, "*Dios mío*. What a waste."

Ramos noticed the coroner watching him silently and had the feeling he was being judged and found wanting. Whatever Martin was thinking, his voice betrayed nothing. "She certainly wasn't a street person. She was clean, well fed, and healthy before her death."

The coroner turned away and pointed his camera at the woman's body, the flash momentarily blinding Ramos. "Once Taylor gets here with the wagon, we can bag her and take her downtown."

Ramos nodded. "Let me go check with the uniforms. I'll meet you at the morgue once I finish up here."

Martin gave a dismissive nod and returned to his work.

Ramos's thoughts drifted to his daughter, Maria, getting ready to head off to college next year. He didn't look forward to telling this woman's parents their daughter had been murdered.

Ramos's thoughts were interrupted by raised voices from the alley's entrance, just beyond the yellow police tape. He saw two uniformed officers arguing. One was Samantha Meyers, a short, wiry woman who had taken more than her share of shit from her fellow officers for being small and female. The other officer, a broad-shouldered bull of a man, was Jake Clement.

Standing between them was a shabbily dressed child. Ramos headed toward them, cursing silently at Clement's presence. The last Ramos had heard, Clement had been assigned to a semi-permanent desk job after getting drunk at last year's holiday party and complaining about all the "wetbacks" in the department. Ramos had left the LAPD because of cops like Clement.

The first time Ramos had met Clement set the tone for their professional relationship. Clement had suggested that Ramos be careful, or ICE would deport him. Ramos responded that returning to Los Angeles wouldn't be so bad but Clement should understand you couldn't be deported if you were a US citizen. He'd added sympathetically that inbred hillbillies probably had trouble understanding such complicated concepts. After that, their interactions were at best, coldly polite.

Ramos reached them as Clement was trying to browbeat Meyers. "This dirty little street rat has no place here. If you'd stop giving in to your fucking maternal impulses, you'd be trying to get rid of him as well!"

Meyers bristled at Clement. "I don't know what's more pathetic, that you're trying to bully a child or that you're such a stupid prick that you think your bullying would work on me."

Ramos glanced at the dirty, gaunt boy who was probably no older than eight. The child looked up at him with large, haunted eyes but said nothing.

Clement noticed Ramos. "If it isn't Detective Ramos, the department's great Latin lover. I heard you and the missus were supposed to be having a hot date tonight."

Ramos fought the urge to punch Clement in the mouth. "Why don't you go help the officers working over in front of the club? You are on the clock, right? Or are you just here to be an asshole?"

Clement gave one of his shit-eating grins, a mock salute, and did what he was told. Ramos watched Clement leave. *Pendejo.*

Meyers sighed. "What a douchebag."

The child suddenly spoke. "Is there a dead person down there?"

Ramos crouched so he was at eye level with the boy. "What's your name, son?"

The child looked blankly at him long enough that Ramos started feeling uneasy. "I can't tell you. It's a secret."

Something definitely wasn't right about this kid. "Do you know anything about what happened down the alley?"

The child leaned forward and whispered, "Beware of the dead woman. She will bring you nothing but sorrow." Before Ramos could respond, the child turned and ran.

"Hey, wait!" Meyers yelled, sprinting after the fleeing child. They disappeared around the corner. Ramos waited until Meyer reappeared, scratching her head. When she reached Ramos she said apologetically, "Damnedest thing, Detective. That little boy just vanished. I lost sight of him for a second or two, and then he was gone."

Ramos was disappointed but tried to sound indifferent. "Well, have the other officers keep an eye out for him. He might have seen something."

Ramos turned to head back down the alley when Meyers pointed upward. "By the way, Detective, what do you make of that? Noticed it just before the kid showed up."

She was pointing at a burned-out emergency light above them, and Ramos could see something hanging from it. He squinted but couldn't quite make out what it was. "Meyers, could you go grab one of the forensics team."

Before Meyers could even turn to leave, whatever was hanging above them was suddenly falling. Ramos grabbed reflexively and caught it before it hit the dirty asphalt. It was a medallion hanging from a pewter chain. It was made of a slate-gray metal, roughly four inches across, and etched with intricate glyphs and pictographs. Ramos had the feeling he'd need a college professor to make heads or tails of where it had come from.

Meyers seemed as perplexed as Ramos. "Think it belonged to the victim?"

Ramos shrugged. "I suppose it's possible. How'd it get up there, though?"

Then a panicked scream echoed down the alley. "Oh God!"

It took a moment for Ramos to connect the voice with a person: Dr. Martin.

The coroner's tone made Ramos's blood run cold. He broke into a run, absently shoving the strange piece of jewelry into his coat pocket. He could hear Meyers following close behind. Martin was shaking, staring into the dumpster. Ramos followed the coroner's gaze.

The dead woman's body was trembling as she drew in ragged breaths of air.

CHAPTER 2

The Keeper of Shadows

Yuri Zhukova exited the elevator into the brightly lit atrium outside the entrance of the penthouse suite. Across from him, standing next to a pair of ornate mahogany doors, was a muscular Asian man stuffed into an expensive suit. "Mr. Kessler will see you shortly."

Yuri nodded and absently perused the expensive-looking paintings on the wall. He'd never been asked to Kessler's penthouse. In fact, he'd never actually met Kessler face to face. Since he'd been hired three years ago he'd always talked to his employer over the phone. He wondered if this meeting had to do with the dead woman.

Kessler had told him to ignore her when he'd first reported the elusive figure watching the smuggling operation. Yuri had to admit she'd been good, very good. But Yuri grew up never backing down from a fight; he'd been twelve when he'd first killed a man trying to steal his girlfriend.

It had become a personal game of cat and mouse between Yuri and the woman. Then some meddling associate of Kessler had delivered her, gagged and bound. Yuri had felt cheated.

"Mr. Kessler will see you now." The bodyguard's voice snapped him out of his dark reverie. The doors to the penthouse were opened, and a dimly lit foyer waited beyond. Yuri paused before stepping through the doorway. He'd only taken a few steps when the doors shut behind him.

He let his eyes adjust to the subdued lighting and noticed more paintings on the walls and a hallway leading from the foyer. He followed it and found a large room at the end of the hall. Floor-to-ceiling windows filled two of the walls, giving a breathtaking view of the nighttime vista of Silicon Valley. Bookcases covered the remaining walls, filled with worn, leather-bound books.

He flinched when a quiet voice spoke off to his right. "So good of you to take time out of your busy schedule to come see me."

Yuri recognized Kessler's voice; it was calm and melodic, with a quality that forced you to listen whether you wanted to or not. He turned to face the speaker.

Yuri was less than impressed by Kessler's physical appearance. He himself stood six foot eight and weighed in at a muscular three hundred pounds; Kessler was a foot shorter and less than half Yuri's weight. He was dressed in a black business suit, pricey-looking leather shoes, and dark gloves. His skin was the color of alabaster, and his long white hair was pulled back into a ponytail. He wore a pair of stylish wrap-around shades that hid his eyes.

Yuri's immediate reaction was disgust. The man was a weakling, a defective, a fucking albino. Kessler's mouth curved into a smile, and Yuri had the irrational feeling that his mind had just been read.

"Help yourself to a drink, Mr. Zhukova." Kessler motioned graciously to a small bar nearby. Yuri nodded in thanks. He went over and poured himself some vodka, draining his glass in one gulp. He poured another.

On second thought, Kessler didn't appear so much an albino as a corpse. The skin was pulled tightly over his skull, and his lips were a thin, taut line. Yuri drained his second glass.

Kessler watched him silently until Yuri finally managed to ask, "You vanted to see me, Mr. Kessler?"

Kessler moved casually over to a leather chair and sat down. Something detached itself from the shadows next to his seat and skittered up to perch on his shoulder. Yuri couldn't decide if it was a weasel or a large black ferret. He found himself transfixed by the steady stare of its gleaming red eyes as Kessler stroked its fur, speaking to it as if it understood. "What do you think, Kibit? His name is Yuri Zhukova, a veteran of the Russian mafia, imported directly from the roughest slums in Moscow. He's an incredibly strong-willed man, keenly intelligent for someone in his line of work and most importantly, he is completely lacking in human empathy of any kind. That's why I hired him. No qualms about committing theft, torture, rape, or murder."

When Kessler turned his attention back to Yuri, the Russian wasn't sure if he should reply. The thing on Kessler's shoulder opened its mouth and revealed rows of needle-like teeth, and Yuri had the feeling it was smiling at him. Kessler continued stroking its fur.

Yuri drained yet another glass of vodka. "Ve all have our talents, Mr. Kessler."

Kessler gave a humorless laugh. "I suppose so. It's unfortunate following orders isn't one of yours. I've been told you carried out an unsanctioned killing last night. None other than the woman I told you to ignore. Is this correct?"

"Nosy bitch had it coming. It was someone you knew who delivered her. I took opportunity to put end to her game."

Kessler froze, and the thing on his shoulder tensed beneath Kessler's hand. "Someone I knew?"

Yuri swallowed heavily despite himself. "Middle Eastern man in expensive clothes. Called you Keeper of Shadows and said woman vas gift from Pharaoh Club."

Kibit squirmed free of Kessler's grip and disappeared behind the chair. Kessler pondered the news several long moments before he straightened his shoulders, took a breath, and smiled mirthlessly. "It was I who gave you the order, Yuri, and only I could rescind it. Do you have anything to say in your defense?"

Given his employer's icy tone, Yuri felt like he'd just been caught beating up Kessler's grandmother. He refilled his glass with vodka, draining it before responding. "She vas endangering smuggling operation. I decided our profit margin vas more important zan playing games."

Kessler sighed and shook his head dismissively. "The smuggling operation is just an insignificant piece of a much larger picture."

Yuri was speechless. Millions of dollars of contraband moved through the warehouse every week.

"Now one of my greatest hopes for the coming endeavor is almost certainly ruined, thanks to your lack of impulse control. However, there is one way you could redeem yourself, Yuri. Tell me you retrieved her medallion."

Yuri looked blankly at his boss, and an expression of displeasure crossed Kessler's pallid face. "How unfortunate. Now the question is, are you still of any use to me?"

Yuri's mind worked quickly. He wasn't going to wait around for Kessler to summon his hired muscle. Taking the small man hostage might buy him time to get out of the building. He pulled the small automatic pistol concealed beneath his belt at the small of his back.

Before he could even aim it, his employer became an impossible blur of motion.

The next thing Yuri knew, Kessler had swatted the gun from his hand and slammed him into a picture window, which cracked from the force of the impact. The small man's gloved hand was wrapped around Yuri's throat. As hard as Yuri tried, he couldn't dislodge himself.

"Perhaps you're just the person I've been looking for. Are you familiar with Nietzsche? 'And if you gaze long into an abyss, the abyss also gazes into you.' Perhaps I know of something even more monstrous than you, Mr. Zhukova." His employer's voice was calm.

Kessler removed his shades and smiled, looking into the Russian's eyes. When Yuri's mind finally comprehended what was happening, he screamed.

CHAPTER 3

Intro to Intensive Care

She was surrounded by a serene darkness and wondered if she were in the womb or, part of her hoped, dead. She clung to the perfect oblivion as long as she could, but a vague discomfort began intruding. When it became unbearable, she felt an irresistible pull to return to the waking world.

As consciousness returned, the first sensations she processed were noise and pain. What was that damned beeping? Goddess, it made her aching head feel like it was going to crack open. She reached up and touched her temple, discovering her head was wrapped in bandages. This was all wrong. She felt a rising sense of panic.

When she opened her eyes, the dim light of the hospital bay made her want to vomit. She started to choke and realized a breathing tube had been shoved down her throat. She fumbled with it until she managed to yank it out.

The piercing beep was coming from a heart monitor tethered to her by a tangle of wires. She reached over and managed to shut off the obnoxious device without knocking it onto the floor and spent the next several minutes peeling off the adhesive tabs connecting the wires to her pale skin. Then she realized she had IV needles in both her arms. She muttered vague obscenities as she methodically removed the IVs as well. At some point during her struggles a low alarm began sounding somewhere beyond her cubicle.

What was she doing in this hospital bed anyway? She struggled to remember, but her few coherent memories melted like snowflakes when she tried to seize them. The pain in her head was only complicating matters.

Curtains made up the walls of her cubicle, but one set hadn't been entirely closed, allowing her to glimpse a nurse's station beyond.

She tried to sit up and regretted it. Her stomach convulsed, and she began to dry heave over the side of the bed. When the retching finally stopped she rolled onto her back, fading in and out of awareness as pain lanced through her skull.

She was brought back to consciousness when she heard voices at the nurses' station. She could see a big man in a police uniform and a nurse with striking Nordic features and golden blond hair wound into a bun. "Damn it officer. That's why I wanted to you stay here in case a patient alarm went off. I already told you we're short staffed tonight."

"We were only gone a few minutes! I didn't hear you complaining when I was following you," he bellowed.

The nurse glared at the big policeman. "Keep your voice down Officer Clement! This is an intensive care unit, not a brothel—in case you were confused."

He crossed his beefy arms. "Very funny."

The woman heard the nurse sigh, "The patient alarm is from your injured woman again. That's the fifth one tonight. Maybe you should just sit down in your chair over there and do you job."

The big man leaned forward and the injured woman noticed the alarm went silent. "Don't tell me how to do my job. I've been a cop eighteen years. If the damned equipment wasn't so old maybe you'd stop getting these false alarms."

The nurse responded without missing a beat, "Your job? I thought you were here to protect that injured woman, not grab my ass and try to get me to fuck you?"

The big man grumbled angrily, "Okay! Shit, I thought blonds liked sex. Especially hot blonds like you."

She didn't dignify the statement with an answer.

Despite just wanting to fall back onto the bed, the woman licked her lips and swallowed, trying to moisten her throat so she could call out to them. Then she stopped.

"Flee this place. You are in terrible danger. He's coming."

She looked around to see who had whispered the warning, but no one was nearby. Wonderful—she'd also lost her mind. Then adrenaline was coursing through her, the sense of urgency forcing her to full awareness. She was just glad no one had noticed her heart monitor was off, heard her earlier attempts to throw up, or bothered checking on whatever alarm she'd set off. Right now, she doubted the two people glaring at each other at the nurses' station would notice if she exploded.

She tried to sit up again. This time, the nausea didn't overwhelm her and the agony in her head was manageable.

She slid off the bed and onto the floor. The linoleum was icy against her bare feet, and her legs wobbled, threatening to collapse beneath her. She held onto the bed and braced herself, waiting for her legs to steady.

Other than the bandages around her head, the only thing she was wearing was a drafty hospital gown, but modesty was the least of her worries right now.

She crept through the curtains just as the big policeman shouted at someone unseen, "Who are you? Stop where you are, or I'll shoot!"

*****

Clement was pissed at the nurse after she'd finished her monologue. He'd been so sure a goddess like her would want to get some with a stud like him. What a stuck-up ice queen.

When the doors to the ICU slid open and two figures entered he forgot the nurse and reflexively put his hand on his sidearm.

After getting a better look at the two men, he drew his pistol and leveled it at them. "Who are you? Stop where you are, or I'll shoot!"

One of the men was impeccably dressed with a creepy smile on his pasty white face. While the first character was unsettling enough, Clement felt menace radiating from the big man next to him. His mouth seemed too wide for his head, and his eyes were an empty, sickly white.

The small man's voice was soft but clear. "Yuri, submit and find her. We finish this tonight."

Clement opened fire. He was one of the top ten police marksman in Central California. All his shots struck the big man center mass in an impressively tight shot group.

The big man smiled, ignoring the bleeding wounds in his chest, and began to change.

*****

Kessler stood silently outside the curtained ICU bay. The Archivist had slipped away.

"Find her, Yuri. She can't have gotten far."

Yuri stiffened at Kessler's tone, but the thing he had become stirred at the sound of Kessler's voice. Yuri's rational mind was crammed into a dark corner of his brain, the Grendel's raging spirit now in control. A ravenous hunger filled him, and he wanted nothing more than to devour human flesh. He glanced over at the broken bodies of the policeman and nurse.

His painfully sharp instincts sensed the prey's scent everywhere. The ICU bay was cramped, the Grendel's shaggy ten-foot frame leaving little room to move. He tore the curtains down and bounded to the reception area. He sniffed the motionless body of the police officer at the automatic doors.

Drool dripped from his fang-filled maw, and he lunged forward, locking his jaws around the policeman's torso. Bones cracked, and a strangled scream escaped the big man's lips as he was crushed. His scream became a gurgle as blood gushed from his mouth. The Grendel shook him, tearing and snapping his corpse into pieces. He quickly gobbled the chunks and turned toward the bloodied, half-conscious nurse.

"Find the Archivist!"

The Grendel tried to resist the command but tore his attention from the shaking woman. The bit of the Grendel's mind that was still Yuri noticed something was missing from the police officer's now mangled gun belt. The Grendel was a creature of both spirit and physical form, all but indestructible. It ignored Yuri's concern.

The beast dropped to all fours and began to follow its quarry's trail. It charged out of the ICU, not waiting for the automatic doors to open. They flew off their track, twisted and broken by the force of the Grendel's impact. When the creature slowed, Kessler was right there, his tone tolerating no delay.

"Find her now!"

The Grendel reluctantly returned to the trail. Her scent led from the ICU toward a door at the end of a long hallway, a glowing green exit sign above it. Yuri felt hunger and rage surge as the body he was trapped in charged forward, sensing its prey was close.

The Grendel tore the heavy metal fire door off its hinges and bounded forward into the stairwell landing. Its keen sense of smell suddenly became a liability. Pepper spray had been liberally doused on the landing and set the beast's nose on fire.

Even as the monster howled in furious agony, Yuri had to give a nod to the woman's cleverness.

Kessler watched silently from the hall, his lips pursed with anger.

*****

The woman listened intently, holding her breath so as not to miss the sound of footfalls or that shambling hell-beast she'd left the puddle of pepper spray for. All was silent.

She was thankful that Dr. Anita Gibson (at least that was the name on the door) had left her fourth-floor office unlocked.

She was crouched underneath the office desk, concealing herself as she rummaged through the doctor's gym bag. She smiled when she realized she'd hit the jackpot: sweat pants, a black t-shirt, a hoodie, socks, and running shoes. She yanked off her hospital gown and began pulling on her new clothing, but her good mood evaporated quickly— Dr. Gibson was considerably shorter and heavier than she was. After several awkward attempts at putting on the clothes, she settled for just adequately covering herself with them. The legs of the sweat pants only reached mid-calf, and the t-shirt and hoodie hung loosely on her, leaving her midriff partially exposed. The socks were snug but fit. The shoes were a lost cause, far too small for her feet.

"Of all the pathetic luck," she muttered to herself.

Despite her shabby ensemble, she steeled herself to emerge from under the desk and escape the hospital.

Just then the door to the office swung open. From her vantage point, all she could see was someone's leather dress shoes taking three silent steps into the office.

"Where are you, Archivist?" The voice was quiet, thoughtful. She held her breath, though blind terror made her want to scream. The speaker advanced, nearing the point where he would step around the desk and see her.

Then the chiming of a cell phone broke the tension. His advance faltered and then stopped. She heard a beep and an annoyed voice. "This is Kessler."

The murmur of the caller's voice could be heard in the stillness of the room.

When Kessler answered, the barely contained anger underlying his words hung thick in the air. "I don't know what your game is, Hamad, but she's slipped away. In any case, you won't stop what's coming, and the Pharaoh Club won't protect you either."

Another beep, and the call ended. The leather shoes lingered in her line of sight briefly before they turned and departed. She listened to the sound of his footfalls grow fainter in the outside hall, gasping for air only when she was certain he was gone. She left her cover and crept out of the office, ready to find the way out of the hospital.

CHAPTER 4

The Dancing Hut

Business at the Dancing Hut was slow tonight, unlike the previous evening when cops had been crawling all over the place because of the murder across the street. Josef Serkin, the bartender and owner of the club, watched Lily gyrating slowly around her pole on stage as he leaned against the empty bar. She appeared tired and sick. He needed to start looking for a new dancer.

The air reeked of stale cigarette smoke, beer, and vomit. He considered getting out the mop bucket and slopping some disinfectant around to cut the smell but didn't feel like making the effort.

In addition to Lily on stage making love to her pole, a few regulars—most of them chronic alcoholics, perverts, or both—sat at tables by the stage and drank while ogling the naked dancer's gyrations. Then there was Lawrence, a local drug dealer, working out of a booth near the restrooms. Lawrence paid him a small fee for the privilege. Lily would be seeing him for her fix once her shift was done.

In retrospect, he was glad he'd inherited the club from his father eighteen years before. At first he'd refused to take over the rundown club despite his dying father's wishes. In the end, his domineering father had prevailed. Josef had to admit that, over time, the place had grown on him.

His great-grandfather had opened the place back in the 1920s. Grigory Serkin was an odd bird who'd fled Russia during the Revolution back in 1917. Stories persisted, fueled by Grigory's own inebriated ramblings, that the reason he'd fled had had nothing to do with the bloody civil war tearing his country apart. He'd fled because of something he'd seen while hunting in the forests outside Tsaritsyn.

The story was that Grigory, while out hunting, had stumbled across a remote forest clearing containing a surreal scene. Inside a fence constructed of human bones was a medieval peasant's hut. As if the human bones hadn't been terrifying enough, the hut had been dancing like a grotesque marionette on giant bird legs. As the story went, Grigory had caught a glimpse of a horrific face watching him from one of the windows, though the exact description changed each time he retold the story. Grigory had run until he'd passed out from exhaustion. When he awoke, he'd been holding one of the skulls from the bone fence.

Supposedly it was the same skull sitting on a dusty shelf behind the bar. Josef, a hulking ex-boxer, spent as much time telling stories about his glory days in the ring as he did about his family's strange patriarch and the skull.

Then one of his regulars came into the club and headed to the bar. Everyone grew quiet for a moment, watching him until he sat down. The man fit in like an elephant at a dog show.

"The usual, Josef," he said casually, his suit, gold watch, and jeweled rings probably worth more than the entire damned club. He was Middle Eastern, well past retirement age, going gray at the temples. He had sharp, aquiline features and always had an enigmatic smile on his lips. Josef had never been able to learn the man's name and he gave the club's owner the creeps.

Josef brought out the special brandy he kept under the bar and poured the man a glass, leaving the bottle. Josef went about his business, knowing the rich man would now just sit, sipping his drink and staring into space until the bottle was empty. What Josef failed to notice was that the nameless man always stared in the direction of the dusty skull on the shelf.

CHAPTER 5

Out on the Town

It was evening, and the nameless city's skyline was alive with lights. The ill-fitting clothes she'd liberated from the hospital were chafing in all the wrong places. Talcum powder would have been nice—or just a bottle of whiskey so she'd cease caring.

She found herself in a rundown industrial neighborhood with empty, weed-choked lots; cracked pavement; rusty remains of abandoned cars; and an assortment of gang tags spray-painted here and there. Knots of people cautiously crossed the streets, heading, she assumed, for less ominous neighborhoods. She considered asking someone for help or just some basic information about where she was.

The first person she approached, a paunchy, middle-aged man absorbed by his cell phone, cut her off before she finished her first word. "No spare change." He went around her and walked briskly onward.

The next few attempts to talk with someone were met with silence or similar muttered excuses, followed by hurried retreats. She finally gave up after the last woman hurled an empty water bottle at her and screamed, "Get a job you fucking parasite!" She wondered if people would be more willing to talk to her in a nicer neighborhood.

This part of the city seemed permeated by sadness and anger. She saw the first ghost huddled in a doorway. There were other spirits, sitting in parked cars, standing on corners with a hand held out, or walking slowly down the sidewalks. Their spectral attire, mismatched and worn, marked most of the deceased as homeless people. Along with the restless dead, she found she could sense faint mystical patterns running through the ground, up the buildings, anchoring the ghosts to this place, and connecting to more energetic patterns elsewhere in the city.

The living had vibrant auras, their color and shape determined by the person's health, emotional state, and subtle interactions with other people.

These distractions were interesting but didn't change her current situation. She still couldn't remember who she was, where she lived, or how she'd ended up in this unfamiliar city. The one thing she could say for certain was that she was hungry. Her stomach growled, and a wave of dizziness mingled with the pain in her head. She would have given the clothes off her back for a stale bagel. Given how crappy her clothes were, it didn't seem like a particularly fair trade, though.

The woman caught her reflection in an intact store window and was sorely disappointed at the severe, tired face looking back at her. She was reminded of a drug addict who needed a fix: sickly, pale, and exhausted. The bandages around her head and ill-fitting clothes only added to the picture of pathetic destitute. It was no wonder people wouldn't talk to her. She stood pulling at her clothes until she felt slightly less exposed and then pulled up the hood of her sweats to hide the bandages swaddling her head.

The light-studded skyline she'd seen earlier was closer now. She continued toward it, reasoning that the high-rises probably meant a better part of the city. She felt as if she were being watched by unseen eyes in this neighborhood. She pressed stoically onward, as much to keep her sock-clad feet warm as to reach some sign of normal activity— restaurants, nightlife, or even a church or soup kitchen. Then she saw a large, garishly lit liquor store not too far ahead. People drifted in and out before heading wherever they were going. On the cross street beyond the store, cars drove by. As before, no one paid her any attention, but the sight of other people who appeared to be just living their lives was somehow comforting.

Two drunks outside the store hurled insults and ineffective punches at each other. A voice nearby bellowing for Monique to get her ass somewhere right now caused her head to ache, and a driver blowing a horn at a jaywalker made it hurt even more.

Then someone grabbed her from behind and slammed her face first into the brick wall. Her head exploded in pain yet again, and for a moment she feared she would black out. Through the waves of throbbing agony she was faintly aware of being dragged out of sight into a small, empty parking lot. She was spun around, and her arms were pinned behind her back.

A dark-haired man in a cheap suit chuckled as he looked her up and down. "You're not Monique. Shit, I need glasses. You are a nice piece of ass, though."

Though the man in front of her was a few inches shorter than her, she could tell the one holding her arms from behind was larger and stronger.

The small man licked his lips. "You look down on your luck, baby. Tell you what, I'll buy you some dinner if you give me and Chuck here blow jobs. What do you say?"

The man behind her laughed. "Good one, Sidney."

She tried to comprehend their words, but her thoughts were a painful muddle. A "blow job"? Was that some sort of exotic massage technique that involved her punching them?

Apparently taking her confused silence as interest, Sidney's eyes glinted hungrily. "Hell, throw in a gang bang as well, and I'll even get you a room for the night."

What was this man's fascination with being hit? Food and shelter sounded like heaven, but part of her was repulsed by these men.

Then Sidney reached up under her T-shirt and groped her breasts. What happened next was a blur, so automatic she didn't even think about what she was doing. Chuck let out a scream and released her arms. As she pulled away, she saw her hands were wreathed in blue flame. She slammed a fist into Sidney's face and felt his jaw dislocate. His hair singed as he flew through the air and fell sprawling across a handicapped parking space. With Sidney no longer defiling her with his touch, she spun around and drove her knee into Chuck's crotch as hard as she could. She heard something pop, and Chuck let out a high-pitched scream and crumpled to the ground.

The two men moaned and whimpered. She did a quick visual scan to make sure no one was coming to their aid and stopped breathing—approaching, though still several blocks away, she saw a hulking shadow with a pair of leprous white eyes glowing in the dark.

Oh Goddess, that hell-beast was still after her! The blue fire wreathing her hands went out, and she took off at a sprint, not looking back. She'd run several blocks before it dawned on her she was heading away from where the crowds of people were, not toward them. Then she heard screams coming from where she'd left Sidney and Chuck, followed by a thunderous, inhuman roar that echoed through the darkening streets.

She picked up the pace, using her fear-induced adrenaline to overcome her exhaustion. It seemed every time she slowed she thought she heard claws scraping against asphalt, heard sniffing noises in the distance, or felt the monster watching her. She needed to keep a clear head, but it was so hard.

She darted between tall buildings and into another street. Suddenly she was blinded by headlights and deafened by the sound of screeching tires.

CHAPTER 6

Cold Case Blues

R amos stood in front of the vending machine, finally deciding on a granola bar for breakfast. As the machine whirred and dropped his selection, he stretched and yawned. It was nearly dawn and the homicide case he'd started last night had blown up into something more.

He'd nearly reached home when he'd overheard a call regarding a disturbance at the ICU and rushed to the hospital. The woman found in the dumpster was gone, Officer Clement was missing, and the only apparent witness was an unconscious nurse found at the scene, Joanna Pryce. She'd suffered multiple broken bones, internal injuries, and an inexplicable loss of blood.

The chief of hospital security, a Marine veteran named Richard Mahoney, reported that the ICU security footage from the time in question had been deleted. He was working on recovering a backup from an unsanctioned computer he'd set up for just such an emergency. Ramos got the feeling Mahoney was more than a little paranoid.

While the ICU was cordoned off and being picked over by a forensics team, Ramos started questioning some of the hospital personnel.

The surgeon who had operated on the not-dead woman from the dumpster, one Dr. Harris, had offered little useful information. During the surgery he'd extracted three fragmented bullets from the woman's brain. He could give no medical explanation for how she could have survived such injuries. He'd also found an object that had been inserted into the wound after she'd been shot. He'd shown it to Ramos: a black, seven-inch thorn or animal tooth. Ramos had bagged it as evidence and put it in his pocket.

None of it made any sense. DNA and fingerprint searches on the woman had so far all come back negative. He was finding himself faced with more questions than answers.

When he was informed that the comatose nurse, Joanna Pryce, had come to, he'd hurried to her room to talk to her. Despite being conscious, she was so drugged up that she'd only cried, screamed, and rambled on about monsters.

Ramos headed to the hospital's security room to see if Mahoney had downloaded his illegal 'backup' yet.

Mahoney was sitting at the hospital's security console, and Ramos could see a download bar on one of the computer screens that was nearly finished.

Mahoney glanced at him and shook his head, "Took longer than I'd planned but here we go, all set."

Mahoney accessed the footage and advanced it to the time in question. As the footage began to play, the first thing Ramos noticed was Nurse Pryce and Sergeant Clement were not at the nurses' station. After a few minutes Pryce appeared with Clement close behind, even though he was supposed to have been guarding the victim, not trailing after the nurse. Pryce and Clement were obviously arguing, though since the security footage had no sound, the subject was unclear.

As Clement and the nurse talked heatedly, two figures entered the ICU. The bigger of the two stepped forward and stopped just short of the nurses' station. An out-of-focus figure hung back near the doors. Clement drew his gun, leveled it, and yelled something at the new arrivals.

When the big man stepped forward, Clement opened fire. The big man flinched with each shot, but that was all. Maybe he was wearing body armor.

Then he *changed*.

As he grew larger, his clothing tore away, revealing a pelt of dark, coarse hair; his arms became so long they nearly dragged the floor, and his face twisted into a nightmarish parody of a man, with shark-like teeth and soulless white eyes. The thing lunged forward, smashing through the reception counter, swatting the nurse aside and throwing Clement over its shoulder as if he were a rag doll.

"What in God's name ..." Ramos gasped, almost choking on his mouthful of granola. The second figure refused to come into focus. Even when it began moving, the ghostly blur traveled with it.

Then he saw the woman from the dumpster darting out from a hiding place and circling around the nurses' station in the opposite direction of the intruders. She moved like a shadow despite the awkward hospital gown and bandages swaddling her head. She stopped at Clement's prone form, his body keeping the automatic doors to the ICU from closing, and snatched something from his belt before exiting, a step ahead of her pursuers who had yet to realize she wasn't in her bed.

"Is there any chance this footage has been altered?"

Mahoney shook his head. "I don't see how. Someone deleted the original footage but this was stored on a secure computer elsewhere. It couldn't have been accessed by anyone but me."

"Then can you explain what we're seeing here? I mean, how is any of this shit possible?"

The security chief seemed to be at a loss, shrugging his shoulders. "I don't know ..."

Then the shaggy beast began eating Officer Clement alive, tearing him limb from limb. Once it had finished, only bloody bits of Clement's clothing and the contents of his mangled gun belt were left. "Good God," Mahoney moaned before turning away and vomiting into the waste paper basket.

Ramos was speechless, tossing what was left of his granola bar into the garbage pail Mahoney was using.

Then after pausing near the nurse, the monster crashed through the now shut automatic doors, bending the metal tracks and doorframe as he went.

The blurred figure moved toward the destroyed doors but paused for several seconds hunched over Nurse Pryce before continuing on after the shambling horror.

Then a hand reached from behind and shut the surveillance footage off.

"Detective Ramos, we'll take it from here."

Both Ramos and Security Chief Mahoney jumped. Behind them were two men in suits and long raincoats.

The taller man held out a badge. "Special Agent Travers, FBI. This is Special Agent Garcia. We're taking over this investigation."

Ramos stood up and squared his shoulders. "This is a local homicide investigation," he said, his voice angrier than he wanted. "You'll have to talk to my superiors before you waltz in here and try to—" He broke off when Garcia held up the proper paperwork, signed by the police commissioner herself.

"In any case, Detective, there's no homicide to investigate. The woman you thought was dead is in fact alive, correct? There's no need for your expertise here." Travers's tone was officious, but his expression smacked of smug arrogance that pissed Ramos off even more.

"What about Officer Clement? He was torn apart," Ramos nearly screamed at the men.

"The details of Clement's disappearance have yet to be verified. Now it's time for the big boys to take over and finish this all up," Travers explained in a patronizing voice.

Ramos tried to form a properly sarcastic response, but faced with the commissioner's signature, there was nothing he could do. Without a word he gathered his coat and left the hospital security console, Security Chief Mahoney, and the two federal agents behind.

This wasn't the last they'd hear from him though.

CHAPTER 7

Alex

A lex Monroe's mouth twitched as he was verbally assaulted by the diminutive old man standing before him.

"I returned that book on time! I'm not paying that ridiculous fine! Yer nothing but a bunch of *Nazis!*"

Alex felt the last shred of his customer service civility evaporate. His nerves were already frayed. So far today he'd had to mop up puke in the public restroom, throw out a woman he caught cutting pages out of a library book, and endure a pointless two-hour meeting where his absence wouldn't have been noticed.

Now, with only twenty minutes before the end of his shift, the elderly patron nicknamed "the Professor" by the staff was well into one of his incoherent rants. The Nazi bit was the last straw for Alex.

When the man paused to take a breath, Alex cut him off. "Nazis? The staff of the Franklin Branch Library are *Nazis?* With all the time you spend here I would think you'd be better acquainted with world history. I suggest that before you vomit forth your mind-shattering ignorance and wallow in it like a pig, you go to the history section and actually read a book on Nazism! If you don't want to be bothered, I'll be happy to retrieve some books for you. As for the fines, you always return your items late! If you don't want fines, bring your books back *on time!*"

At some point during the tirade his attempt at keeping his voice library-quiet had failed, and now he was shouting.

It had grown dead quiet, something unusual for the Franklin Branch Library. All the people socializing or lounging and even the rare few reading had frozen, staring at him with expressions of surprise, shock, and amusement.

The professor stared blankly at him for a moment and then backed away until he'd reached the lobby. Without another word, he turned and fled.

"Mr. Monroe! Come to my office immediately," a voice commanded. It was Miss Bidmire, the branch manager, who he'd thought had left early like she always did. The plump woman's face was dangerously red when he entered her office.

Alex let her rail on for ten minutes before responding to her outraged accusations and reminders of his past infractions.

"So let me get this straight, Miss Bidmire. Now we're just supposed to stand there and let people call us Nazis?"

Miss Bidmire took a deep breath, her voice less shrill, "I didn't say that. But there are better ways of dealing with such things, Mr. Monroe. Your sarcastic, knee-jerk reaction when people are less than polite has no place in a public library! I need to decide what I'm going to do with you." She held her head as if she'd just developed a severe headache.

As Alex left Bidmire's office, he wanted to scream or cry or do both at once. His coworkers and patrons once again stared at him. He bowed with a flourish. "Thank you, thank you! Catch me tomorrow for another performance, assuming I'm not fired."

He turned and marched outside, stopping at the commemorative bench near the library's entrance. He read the bronze plaque. "Dedicated to Benjamin Franklin, Founder of America's Public Libraries." He wondered what Ben Franklin would think of public libraries in the twenty-first century? From what Alex had seen, he didn't think Ben would be too happy.

He saw Jen's battered old Toyota parked on the other side of the street, the streetlight illuminating her face and red mane of hair as she read a book while waiting to pick him up.

He hesitated, realizing his foul mood wasn't just because of work. His father's phone call last night had sunk him into a fuming depression. He'd barely let his father speak, losing his temper and venting his pent-up anger before hanging up abruptly.

His father had remained silent for four years, ever since their final screaming match the Christmas Eve before Alex had moved out. He'd never been particularly close to his father, and after his mother had died in the accident, his father's attempts to be a parent while dealing with the war injuries incurred during his stint in the army were less than stellar. The pain medications were worse than alcohol, and the night Alex had left his father had said things he couldn't take back and that Alex couldn't forgive, including implying that Alex was the reason his mother was dead.

Alex had packed and left the following morning. He'd been determined to prove to his father he could make it on his own. He wouldn't have lasted long if not for Jen, his long-time neighbor and level-headed best friend, coming with him into his self-imposed exile.

He took a deep breath and tried to calm down. He waited until it was clear, then crossed the street and slipped into the passenger seat of Jen's car.

"So, how was your day," he asked in an overly cheerful voice.

She looked at him and rolled her eyes. "My day was great. Got a fifty-dollar tip from some rich dude who liked how I mixed his Manhattan. You on the other hand—"

Alex slumped. "Probably going to get fired. I lost my temper and screamed at a patron," he muttered despondently.

He was ready for her to remind him this wasn't the first such incident, but she just patted him on the shoulder. "So what else is new. Tell you what, let's splurge and order pizza tonight. We'll put my tip to good use, and after we eat, I'll forgo reading to stay up late watching one of your lousy sci-fi movies with you."

Feeling better already, he grinned. "Don't you think it's funny that I work at a library and am addicted to movies, while you work at a bar and are constantly reading books?"

She started up the car. "Hilarious. Buckle up and keep smiling."

The car pulled away from the curb and Alex held on as Jen headed up the nearest highway onramp. With the engine rattling, she slowly merged into the unusually heavy evening traffic on I-101.

Alex was about to comment when Jen muttered to herself, "More traffic than usual tonight. Time for a shortcut."

They got off the highway at the next exit, heading home via back roads and surface streets. Alex watched the dark streets pass and left the driving to Jen. She didn't appreciate backseat drivers.

Alex checked his seatbelt as they accelerated down a long, desolate stretch of road. Jen was soon exceeding the speed limit by double digits. Suddenly a figure ran out in front of the car. Alex braced himself as Jen slammed on the brakes; he knew they were too close to stop in time.

CHAPTER 8

Mysteries

"Well, if anyone in their ivory towers would ever tell us dumbasses on the street what was going on, we wouldn't fall for things like this!" Ramos was furious, and even Captain Vaughn was taken aback by his anger.

"No one's blaming you—" the captain began in his most diplomatic tone.

"Then why isn't the commissioner having *her* ass chewed off? She's the one who hands out our cases to the feds like Halloween candy!"

"Listen, no one's chewing your ass off. We need to find out who those men were and what they were after. Was there anything on the security footage that might have helped?"

Ramos was at a loss. Without the footage, what was he supposed to say—*just a monster and a blurry guy?* Whoever those two faux feds were, they'd expunged the restored footage. The hospital's security chief had conveniently forgotten what he'd seen, and the statement from the injured nurse was written off as hysterics.

"Nothing. Just showed our victim sneaking out of the ICU as the masked intruders came in. However, the tape did show Officer Clement being killed. It's all in my report."

Captain Vaughn began tapping his fingers on the desk. "That's unfortunate. Didn't like Clement but he was a fellow cop. The strange thing is those men *were* federal agents, but they've been missing for nearly a year. They bluffed their way into the evidence room yesterday as well, though nothing appears to have been taken. They were looking for something. That woman is the key to all this. If we could find her, maybe we could figure out what's going on."

Ramos's anger gave way to weary resignation. "Easier said than done, Captain. I'll need some extra men to canvas the places she might have hung out. She didn't get her physique eating donuts."

The captain nodded. Then the phone rang, and he motioned that their meeting was over.

Ramos went back to his desk and closed his eyes. His wife had left a voicemail saying she'd decided to finalize their divorce. Now this crap.

His phone rang and he answered when he saw it was dispatch, "This is Detective Ramos."

"We've got two dismembered bodies at De La Cruz Boulevard and Perry Court. Looks like an animal tore them apart."

Ramos rubbed his eyes, "Yeah, sure. On my way."

Ramos hung up and grabbed his coat, unable to expunge the image of Clement being eaten on the security tape. Maybe this was connected to the missing woman.

He'd been on duty for fifteen hours, and it looked like he would be for at least a few more. He headed to the garage and stopped to enjoy a cigarette before he left. It was only then, when reaching into his coat pocket in search of a lighter, that he discovered the amulet he'd found at the crime scene. Looking at the dull, unremarkable piece of jewelry, he felt his stomach sink. Somehow he knew this was what the feds had been trying to find.

CHAPTER 9

A Tedious Conversation

S he stood in a shadowy library, surrounded by a maze of towering bookshelves that looked like they'd been struck by a major earthquake. Books, scrolls, stone and metal tablets, as well as a staggering assortment of other written materials, were strewn randomly on the shelves and floor. She guessed she was dreaming, but everything seemed so real. She reached down and picked up a leather-bound journal, opening it up to a random page. It was written in archaic French. She suddenly wondered how she knew it was archaic French or why could she understand it? She began reading and as she did, a memory flared to life.

She was in a rowboat with Francois, her paramour, an officer in Napoleon's Grand Army. She felt the cool breeze on her face, could hear the honking of the geese, even feel the first pangs of motion sickness accompanying the gentle rocking of the boat on the lake. Her heart was filled with love for her companion. She knew this would be the last time she would see him—he would die in battle at Austerlitz—and she was struck with agonizing sorrow.

She slammed the journal shut and threw it back onto the floor as if it were going to bite her. What the hell was that?

She pushed forward through the aisles, stepping over the treasure trove of books around her. Despite the familiarity and comfort she felt here, she still had no sense of where she was. She could have spent the rest of eternity lost here, but as soon as that thought crossed her mind, she stepped into an open area at the center of the maze.

Antique tables and chairs were neatly arrayed around the circular area. Unlike the dim aisles, this area was brightly lit, though she couldn't say where the light was coming from. Before the center table stood a tall figure. She did a double-take and realized whoever it was looked just like her. Then again, as she moved forward, she could see there were differences.

The stranger's eyes were blank silver orbs. She could see her face reflected in their mirrored surfaces and waited for some profound, cosmic revelation. Her only epiphany was that she looked tired.

The stranger's raven-black hair was a flowing mane that covered her shoulders and spilled down to just above her ankles, quite different from her own short bob.

The impressive figure was clad in a white silk shift that clung to the ample contours of her body.

All right, the woman didn't look *exactly* like her; the silver-eyed woman definitely had more curves.

The stranger's voice was soothing but still conveyed an undertone of disappointment. "You are lost, Archivist. You have no idea who you are. You don't even know who I am."

"Are you going to tell me, or are we going to play twenty questions?"

The stranger tilted her head and looked exasperated. "You may call me Ayesha. We shall call you Rose for now."

"Rose, Daisy, Nightshade, Hemlock, what does it matter? Do I have a *real* name?"

"You've had many names, but Rose was a name you were most fond of. Trust me."

But she didn't trust this almost-but-not-quite doppelganger. For that matter, she didn't trust anyone right now. Not after the hospital, Sidney and Chuck, or the thing that was hunting her.

"Fine, I'm Rose. Do I have a last name, or am I some sort of rock star?"

"Your uncharacteristic sarcasm is not helping matters! We don't have much time. The Twilight Veil will part on the next full moon, and the Keeper of Shadows intends to guide Grandmother through and release her upon this world."

Rose sighed at the cryptic references and threw her hands up in frustration. "Who is Grandmother? What is the Twilight Veil? For that matter, who is the Keeper of Shadows? Goddess, all we need to do is throw in a Bigfoot sighting, and we'll have a best seller in the 'what the fuck' section of the library."

Ayesha's expression was angry, but her voice remained calm. "The Keeper of Shadows, who is also known as Kessler, was the man who came to the hospital to kill you. Long ago he was tasked with keeping those who dwelt beyond the Twilight Veil from passing through into this world. Grandmother is one of these entities. Unlike the others, who require a human host to exist in this physical world, her power has become so great that she is able to manifest physically here without a host."

Suddenly Rose didn't feel so flippant, an ominous memory rising in the back of her mind. "A witch. Grandmother is a witch."

Ayesha nodded. "Not just a witch but a spirit given identity and form by all those women throughout history who were unjustly persecuted, tortured, and murdered by men who feared their understanding of the Art. Grandmother's form in this world is that of Baba Yaga, the most terrible witch of Russian folklore."

Rose was silent, a nameless dread causing her to grow cold. Even though the memory was nebulous, she was filled with terror hearing the name.

Ayesha's voice softened. "This place is your sanctuary and a mirror of the state of your mind. As you can see, it is in disarray. I shall soon begin trying to put things in order. Once you return to the waking world, you must seek your key. You will need it if you are to have any chance of stopping what is to come."

Rose was gripped by frustrated anger. "Goddess, how am I supposed to find a lost key and stop that thing? I don't even know who I am!"

Ayesha rose to her full height, and a nimbus of blinding radiance engulfed her. When Rose's eyes recovered she saw Ayesha now had vast wings of pure light. She was clothed in armor of silver scales and held a gleaming sword in one hand. Rose took a step back and wondered what she was—an angel, a Valkyrie, or maybe a spokeswoman for a silver polish company?

Ayesha's piercing voice filled her mind. *You are the Archivist! Stop the Keeper of Shadows from opening the way, or Baba Yaga will plunge this world into eternal despair and darkness!*

CHAPTER 10

Unexpected Guest

M iss Agnes Shaw, landlady of the Riverside Apartments, knocked smartly three times on the tenants' door. The small pug cradled in her left arm, Boozer, gave a low growl.

"I know you two are home," she said irritably, adjusting her flowered muumuu.

She heard a faint noise behind the door, then a chain being undone and a deadbolt being disengaged. She wasn't sure if the stab of irritation showed on her face when she saw it wasn't the polite red-headed girl but Alex, the lanky young man with the boyish, acne-scarred face and the sarcastic mouth. He gave an insincere smile. "So good to see you. How can I help you, Miss Shaw?"

Miss Shaw wished it were Jen, who was so much easier to deal with. She sighed and then put on her most disapproving face. "Another tenant said they saw you bring a drunk woman in earlier. Non-residents exhibiting any sort of public intoxication are not allowed on the property!"

"Your network of spies was actually accurate this time, Miss Shaw. It was a drunk friend who needed a cab. I called one, and she left. You might want to set your nosey nellies on the other rule breakers here in the apartment complex. Like Betty Giles in 4-B with her twelve cats? You can smell the cat piss in the hall. Or maybe Tom Miller in 1-C with his side job selling pirated DVDs? Maybe it's the fact that Betty is your BFF or Tom adds a little something to his rent each month to keep you quiet about his business?"

The pug in her arms growled and yipped at Alex. With Jen he only panted and wagged his tail. Miss Shaw tried to regain her righteous indignation. "That doesn't change the fact that you two need to follow the rules. You signed your lease agreement like everyone else. I'm just—"

Alex interrupted. "If you don't believe me, come in and see for yourself. Then you could fix the leaks in the bathroom we've been waiting three months to have repaired. I even have a tool box you can use."

The landlady took a step back, conceding, "That's not necessary. I'll have a plumber come tomorrow." She refused to give the ill-mannered youth the pleasure of seeing her upset and tried to act calm as she walked away, stiff-backed.

Jen watched Alex slam the door and secure the locks. She was seated in the easy chair, her hands pressed against her face as she tried to control her shaking.

How could Alex be so calm? She tried to expunge tonight's sights and sounds from her mind, but they kept replaying in an endless loop—the sickening thud as the woman cartwheeled over the car, her prone body in the street, and her scraped and bloody face as they ran over to her. The worst was the woman's frantic voice pleading with them to drive away before it was too late.

Jen had pulled out her phone to call 911, but the injured woman had been adamant. "No police, no ambulance. They'll just find me again," she'd explained through clenched teeth.

The urgency in the injured woman's voice had made Jen take charge. She'd helped Alex get the woman up, to the car, and into the back seat before getting behind the wheel. Alex was just climbing into the passenger seat when she saw *something* step out into the street behind them, a block away. It was backlit by a streetlight, a silhouette of a shaggy giant—the Boogey Man who'd hid in her closet when she was a kid. It just stood in the street watching them with pale, luminous eyes.

Jen had never been so scared in her twenty-two years. Only dumb luck saved them; if the car hadn't already done a 180-degree spin when Jen braked to try to avoid hitting the woman, or if the engine hadn't still been running, she knew they would have all died then and there. Jen had punched the gas to put as much distance as she could between her car and the nightmare behind them. As the car gained speed, she'd glanced in his rearview mirror and thought her heart would burst. It was chasing them—and gaining. As the Toyota neared top speed, their pursuer lunged at the car, causing it to lurch with an accompanying sound of ripping metal. The monster's burst of speed thankfully didn't last long, and it fell behind, eventually disappearing from view.

As she'd driven home, Jen had concentrated on keeping calm. She'dsped at fifty and sixty miles an hour down the city streets, thankful the police hadn't pulled her over.

By the time they'd pulled into their parking space at the apartment complex, she had managed to calm down and had almost convinced herself she'd imagined it all. Then, when she got out of the car, she'd seen the four ragged furrows torn into the trunk of her car.

Alex was worried about Jen. He'd never seen her so rattled. He went over and crouched next to her in the easy chair. He tried to sound reassuring, taking Jen's hand and squeezing it. "Everything's going to be fine Jen." He glanced over at the injured woman who was bundled up on the couch. She had some color in her cheeks now and was snoring gently. Alex had wrapped her up in one of his old quilts.

Jen asked quietly from the easy chair, "Is she going to be all right?"

Alex nodded. "She seems to be breathing steadily, has a strong pulse, and she's not bleeding."

He returned to the problem at hand, trying to work out what had happened on that dark street. What had attacked the car? Had it been chasing the woman? If so, why? He initially suspected the woman was some sort of con artist, ready to sue them the minute she woke up. Considering what had happened, though, he conceded that it didn't seem likely.

Alex retrieved a first aid kit from the closet and removed the stained bandages were around the woman's head. She continued to sleep, not even stirring as he worked. Her head was completely shaved and she had a web of stitches on the back of her head. As he looked more closely, he frowned. There were no wounds beneath the sutures. He opened a roll of bandages and rewrapped the woman's head to be safe. He tried to adjust her on the couch so she'd be more comfortable. The woman was too tall to fit, so her legs draped over one of the couch's arms. As he shifted her, Alex found himself staring. For a moment she seemed larger than life, a stalwart heroine from some ancient myth. He suddenly felt self-conscious and went back to kneel next to Jen in the easy chair. "We've done all we can for her. We'll let her rest, and hopefully … well, tomorrow's another day. We need sleep, too, so we can both think straight."

Jen nodded mechanically, and Alex pulled her up out of the chair and guided her to their bedroom. He helped her undress and tucked her in before sliding into his own bed. They both quickly fell asleep, hoping the monsters would keep away.

Jen awoke from a nightmare, sweating and gasping for air. When she saw Alex still sleeping, her panic subsided. The blinds were leaking late-morning light, and Jen badly needed to pee. She slipped out of bed and pulled on her underwear. Alex continued sleeping.

She opened the bedroom door just enough to squeeze through and then shut it quietly behind her. The bathroom was behind the only other door in the short hall; she went in and relieved herself. As she washed her hands, the events of the previous night came fully into focus again: the car hitting the woman and the thing that wanted to kill them. A chill ran up her spine, and she shivered.

She decided to check up on their guest. She only prayed her condition hadn't gotten worse. When Jen walked into what could generously be called their living room, she stopped short as her eyes locked with the injured woman's. She was sitting on the couch wrapped in Alex's old quilt.

"Who are you? Where am I?" Her voice was soft but had an intensity that scared Jen.

The first thing that crossed her mind was she was standing in front of this stranger in nothing but her underwear, but she forced herself to answer, "I'm Jen, well actually Jenna. Jenna Sinclair. We hit you last night when you ran out into the street. You said you didn't want an ambulance or police, so we brought you back to our apartment. Something horrible tried to kill us when we were driving away."

The woman listened intently and, when Jen finished, appeared to relax ever so slightly. "Goddess, I remember now. It was the Grendel that was chasing me. How could it have possibly passed through the veil?"

Jen looked at her blankly, not sure what she meant. The injured woman thought for a moment and then looked back at Jen. "May I have some water and something to eat? I haven't had a chance for either since I woke up in the hospital."

Jen, still self-conscious about her state of undress, nodded and went into the kitchenette where she had a counter between her and the woman. She filled a large plastic cup with water and put it on the kitchen counter. She pulled out a loaf of bread and some fixings for sandwiches from the cabinet. "You woke up in the hospital? What happened?"

As the woman stood to get the cup, Jen noticed a pile of clothing on the floor. It was the shabby outfit their guest had been wearing when they brought her home. Her quilt shifted, and Jen caught a glimpse of her naked body and blushed as she realized the woman was wearing even less than she was.

The woman, apparently unaware of her wardrobe malfunction, drained the cup and placed it back on the counter before answering. "I can't remember what happened. Waking up in the hospital is as far back as I can recall."

Jen refilled the cup with water. "So you have amnesia," she asked, thankful the question didn't sound as stupid as she thought it would.

"I suppose so," the woman conceded before taking the cup and draining it in three gulps. Retrieving the cup and filling it a third time, Jen felt like she was at her bartender job.

Jen finished slapping together a trio of peanut butter and jelly sandwiches and placed them neatly on a paper plate while the woman nursed her third cup of water. When she put the food on the counter, the woman snatched the plate and began eating ravenously.

"I'm going to get some clothes on," Jen offered awkwardly, leaving the woman eating as she returned to the bedroom.

She closed the door behind her, still flustered as she pulled on the rest of her discarded clothes from last night. When she was fully dressed, she went over to wake Alex. He moaned as she lightly shook him. "Alex, our guest is awake."

He sat up, rubbing his eyes. "Awake? Are you sure?"

She nodded eagerly.

Alex hopped out of bed and got dressed while Jen told him about her encounter with the woman.

"Do you think she's telling the truth? About the amnesia?"

Jen didn't hesitate. "Yes, I think she really can't remember anything before the hospital."

Alex had known Jen a long time. She was a good judge of people.

He turned to more practical matters. "Ok. Those clothes she had on didn't look too comfortable. I've got a pair of baggy sweat pants that should fit, and you can give her one of your oversized sleeping shirts. I also have those fleece-lined winter boots I never use. Her feet looked close to my size."

When Jen and Alex finally came out to the living room, the woman was wrapped snugly in the quilt again and had finished the sandwiches.

She scrutinized Alex. "You must be the other half of 'we' from 'we hit you last night.'"

Alex couldn't read the woman's tone or expression so just shrugged and smiled, jabbing his thumb at Jen. "It would really be more accurate to say I was in the car that hit you. She's the maniac."

Jen hit Alex in the chest with her open hand. "Shut up!"

The woman visibly relaxed, and a faint smile touched her lips. She bowed her head. "I'm Rose. I'm sorry you've gotten mixed up in all this. Thank you for bringing me here, though. You certainly saved my life."

Alex watched as Jen smiled and sat down on the couch next to Rose. "That's Alexander Monroe. You can call him Alex."

Alex gave a small wave as he sat in the easy chair.

Jen handed Rose the clothes and boots. "These are for you if you'd like them. They're hopefully more comfortable than what you were wearing."

Rose bit her lower lip as she took the clothes. "That's ... that's very kind. I hate to impose further, but could I use your shower before I put these on?"

Jen helped Rose up and led her to the bathroom. Rose left the quilt on the couch, and an embarrassed Alex made an effort to look everywhere except where their naked guest was.

Jen got Rose acquainted with their tiny bathroom, closed the door behind her, and rejoined Alex. "I'm even more confused than I was before," Jen admitted, picking up the quilt and Rose's discarded clothing and cramming them into the hamper in the hallway.

"At least she doesn't seem to hold a grudge over you running her down," Alex observed snidely. Jen hurled a piece of dirty laundry at him. He laughed and tossed it back. "Just making an observation! No comment on your driving intended."

She gave a mock laugh. "Why don't you try buying your own car, and then you can chauffeur *me* all over town."

"Okay, okay, sorry! Didn't mean to open that can of worms," he said defensively and turned on the television with the remote. He switched to a midday news show, and Jen read sullenly on the couch. They were both silent until they heard Rose opening the bathroom door.

"Oh my," Jen gasped as Rose exited the bathroom. Rose was clean, her scraped skin now unblemished, looking surprisingly good in the clothes they'd given her. The bandages on her head were gone, and she sported a head of thick, raven-black hair in a ragged bob.

Rose looked back at the bathroom as if to see what Jen was concerned about. "I did try to clean up after myself."

"No, your hair! How'd you grow a new head of hair," Jen asked, astonished. She knew she didn't have any wigs lying around.

Rose seemed perplexed by the question. "I just used the Art to accelerate my hair's growth. Did I do something wrong?"

Alex answered, "Not wrong, Rose. Just impossible."

Rose gave a nervous, lopsided smile and then changed the subject. "Did you realize you have a fairy living in bathroom? It has a nest up above the shower."

They both stared blankly at her, neither one having the slightest idea how to answer.

Rose shifted uncomfortably. "I suppose it hides itself with its glamour. By the way, has either of you ever heard of the Pharaoh Club?"

CHAPTER 11

Don't Ride with Strangers

Maria Ramos stood at the bus stop, cursing her boyfriend's hormones. Just because he was her ride didn't give him the right to grope her even after she'd told him to stop. But now she was having second thoughts about taking the bus home. It was dark, and there was no one around. She was thankful for the bright lights at the bus stop but would have preferred a few other people waiting as well. Her father had always taught her to be careful, to trust her gut feeling, and she felt uneasy tonight. It probably had more to do with her parents' pending divorce than anything else.

She'd been sure they would patch things up. Then yesterday, her mother had announced she was moving forward with the divorce and Maria realized how much she'd invested in the idea her parents would stay together. She was still shaken.

She thought her mother was being a bitch. Her father had been a cop when they'd gotten married, before Maria had even been born. Now her mom acted as if he'd pulled some trick. Maria missed her dad, who'd moved into his own apartment when her parents had started having problems. She didn't want to have to commute back and forth for Thanksgiving and Christmas. Unlike her friend Cheryl, who had become jaded about her own parents' divorce, Maria thought the holidays were meaningless without an intact family.

She was so lost in thought that she didn't notice the large black sedan that had pulled up until the driver, an immense man in a black turtleneck sweater and slacks, had exited his vehicle and walked up to her.

"Are you Maria Ramos?" he asked with a heavy Slavic accent.

She looked around and realized that, except for him, she was still alone. Before she could run, he grabbed her arm and pulled her to the car as the back door swung open. Without a word he shoved her roughly into the car. The door slammed behind her before she could scramble back out. She frantically tried to find a way to open the door or window, but there were no handles to be found on the inside.

"I would think the daughter of a police detective would be more aware of her surroundings."

She muffled a scream as she realized she wasn't alone. Sharing the back seat with her was a well-dressed man with oversized, wrap-around sunglasses, a nice suit, and ashen skin.

"What do you want? Let me out, or I'll scream."

The man brushed an errant strand of white hair from his face with his gloved hand and smiled.

As a child, Maria had been traumatized by a snarling dog that had cornered her on the playground. The man's smile reminded her of that day. Her insides shrank, and all she wanted to do was hide. She'd never been so scared in all her life.

The sedan lurched into motion, and they were soon speeding down the empty, late-night streets.

Maria was trying to think. Who were these men? What did they want? "Look, I have some money. Just let me go, and it's yours." She tried to sound confident, but her voice wavered.

Her captor laughed. "I'm afraid money is not something I need. The reason we are bringing you along on this ride is that your father possesses knowledge of an object I wish to obtain. Having his only child should help convince him to cooperate. You are worth nothing to me dead."

He grabbed her arm and pulled her toward him. His grip was even stronger than the big man's had been. When she was next to him, he stared at her for a long moment.

Her fragile composure crumpled. "Please, don't hurt me," she said with a sob.

"Pain is a part of existence. Learn to savor it as you would joy or pleasure," he whispered before leaning forward, his cold lips pressing against her throat. The scream rising in her chest was stopped by the sudden, searing agony in her neck.

CHAPTER 12

The Pharaoh Club

Rose's six-foot frame was wedged across the back seat of Jen's Toyota. Despite her awkward position, she'd seemed comfortable, but after Rose shifted for the third time in ten minutes, Jen apologized. "Sorry, but the seat controls are busted. Both seats are stuck where they are."

At the sound of Jen's voice, the small dog that had followed Rose into the back seat decided to push itself between the driver and passenger seats and climb into Alex's lap.

Alex recoiled as if the pug were a rattlesnake. "Oh man, that's our landlady's drooling little monster. How'd it get in the car?"

Rose sounded apologetic. "He climbed into the car with me. I thought you'd seen him."

Jen was delighted. "Boozer is a sweet little dog. You just need to appreciate the little fella."

Alex snorted in disbelief. "If she finds out we have him, she'll tear up our lease. We'll have to find a new apartment because of this disobedient little fleabag."

Boozer barked at Alex's comment, not deigning to actually look at him.

"Shut up, Boozer," Alex snapped. "I hate the yipping little meatloaf. Maybe I can sneak it back inside when we get back. Or better yet, claim I found him wandering the neighborhood!"

Jen sighed. "I think you're overreacting, Alex."

"Really? This thing is the landlady's child. She's probably already called the police," he moaned, making an effort not to touch the dog.

Jen kept her eye on the road. "We'll cross that bridge when we come to it. Calm down and enjoy the scenery."

By the time they left the sleepy town of Los Gatos and started up Highway 9 into the Santa Cruz Mountains, it was late afternoon.

Clearly trying to ignore the dog in his lap, Alex explained in more detail how he'd heard about the Pharaoh Club. "Yeah, it was about a year ago this short, plump fellow in Ren Faire clothes came into the library asking about this Pharaoh Club. Said he was from out of town and attending some conference there. It took me nearly an hour to track down an address for the place, and I ended up finding it in old property records from the nineteenth century."

Rose shifted, to stretch her legs a little. "You certainly didn't have to drive me there. I could have hitched a ride or something."

Jen laughed. "Probably not the best of ideas in the Santa Cruz Mountains. Anyway, it's the least we can do after hitting you."

Rose dismissed the comment with a wave of her hand. "This name is the only thing I have to go on. My head still hurts, and my memories are still missing. The man who set the Grendel loose on me was talking on his phone, and this club came up in the conversation."

Alex began laughing. "Do you even realize how special you are? I'll admit I thought you were nuts when you mentioned the fairy. I couldn't see it, but Jen claims she did. Given everything else you did, I guess I'll believe her."

Jen scowled at Alex. "Thanks."

Boozer squirmed in Alex's lap and then barked at him.

Alex scowled at the dog and then continued, "Growing your hair back, removing the damage to Jen's car with a wave of your hand, and turning my lucky silver dollar to solid gold! Meaning no disrespect, but you're a sorceress or a witch, right?"

Rose didn't answer immediately and just looked out the window. "I can use the Art. I didn't realize it was something unusual, but I'm uncomfortable with those terms. They cause more harm than good. People twist their meaning, use them as labels to justify inflicting cruelty on others. I only know that I am missing something that would allow me to truly understand my mastery of the Art. I'll need everything I can muster to keep the Twilight Veil secure."

Alex began absently petting Boozer. "The Twilight Veil?"

Rose shifted her position again. "It is a mystical barrier that separates this world from a malevolent realm of formless spirits. At some point this reality and theirs came into contact with each other. Over the centuries, those spirits have been given form and identity by the emotions, beliefs, and myths of the human race. The Twilight Veil was meant to protect this world, but it can sometimes grow weak enough for things to pass into this world. I can't let that happen."

Alex whistled. "All right then."

The twisting, two-lane mountain road was claustrophobic, bordered by clusters of dark oaks and pines dwarfed by redwoods towering above them. Rose watched the scenery pass, catching the occasional glimpse of a roadside creek or hidden mountain cabin. Once the sun finally set, only the road was visible in the car's headlights. Rose tried to stay alert but dozed off as Jen and Alex talked softly up front.

Rose was jolted awake when she slammed into the back of the front seats, the car's tires screeching as Jen stomped on the brakes. The car skidded toward a dark gully on the side of the road, but with a final lurch they stopped just short of pitching into the dark abyss. Jen was gasping for air, clutching the steering wheel so tightly her knuckles were white.

Alex finally said, his voice shaking, "What the hell was that thing? I only caught a glimpse of it. A black cat or … I don't know. It was definitely weird."

Jen whispered as much to herself as Alex, "That was no cat. God, I don't know what it was."

Rose felt eyes watching them from the dark. "Just keep driving. Sitting here isn't safe."

Jen checked her mirrors, then pulled back onto the road, driving noticeably slower than before.

Alex started making small talk with Rose; she wasn't sure if it was to calm her down after the near miss or himself. "We've only been on this road an hour or so. If we stay on it and follow it all the way through the mountains to Felton, we could visit the Bigfoot museum."

Rose was wide awake now and continued staring out the window at the dark. "They sometimes wander from their dimension into this one.

Natural settings still hold a fascination for them, even though they can only stay here for short periods of time."

Alex was looking at Rose with an odd expression but remained silent. Then he turned his attention back to the road, "Jen, that's it on the left!"

Jen slammed on her brakes and skidded across the oncoming lane onto a dirt turnoff.

Jen snapped at Alex, "This car's days are numbered as it is, but this trip is going to do my poor baby in. Don't scream at me at the last second. Be my navigator, and pay attention to the road!"

The headlights revealed an imposing wrought iron fence with a matching gate, on which was mounted a sign.

Pharaoh Club
Wellington Lumber Concern–
Private Property

Alex pointed. "Just like the old records said. That was the name of the company that owned the place back in the 1800s."

Rose popped open the door and freed herself from the tight confines of the back seat. She slid out of the car and stepped onto the gravel and into the cool night air. Only a ragged patch of the starry night sky was visible above them through the canopy of trees. The hair on the back of her neck stood up, and she swung around. For a moment she thought she saw a pair of glowing red eyes watching from the trees across the highway, close to the ground. She thought they were small like an animal's, but they were gone before she could be sure.

Jen rolled down her window and pitched her voice so it would be heard over the running engine. "It looks like there's a call box next to the gate on the right there. See if anyone answers."

Rose located the call box, which was illuminated by the Toyota's headlights. She walked over and pushed the big red button. After she heard a click, she asked tentatively, "Hello, is anyone there?"

As soon as she lifted her finger from the button a male voice responded, "This is private property. No trespassers allowed."

She struggled to remember what Kessler had said on his phone. "I'm here to see Mr. Hamad."

She released the button, but there was only silence.

She waited.

Out of the corner of her eye something caught her attention. A small security camera mounted high on a nearby tree was pivoting toward her, a red light flashing as it did so.

With a metal clank, the gates swung inward. "Please stay on the road until you reach the club, ma'am."

Ma'am? That was unusually polite. She pushed the button one last time as the gate finished swinging open. "Thank you."

Rose returned to Jen's side of the car and leaned down to the open window. "Jen, Alex, you've done more than enough for me. I don't want to drag you any deeper into this. If you want to go home, I'd understand."

She watched Alex and Jen exchanged glances, and then Jen said, "No. We'll stay with you. Even if you don't need our help anymore, I'd like to see this through."

When Alex nodded, Rose admitted to herself how happy she was they weren't leaving. She clambered into the back seat and shut the door. "According to the man on the speaker, we just drive until we reach the club."

They pulled through the open gates, which began closing as soon as the car had cleared them. The gravel road was a narrow black tunnel, bordered by hedges and trees that allowed no view beyond them.

"I couldn't hear what the person on the speaker was saying. Do they know you, Rose?" Jen asked.

"Whoever it was called me ma'am. Maybe I work here or do business with them."

The gravel road seemed to twist and turn far longer than it should have. Just when Rose thought this was some strange trick of geometry and optical illusions, they exited the hedge tunnel and entered a broad, moonlit valley with steep, high sides reminiscent of the Alps. Nestled against the end of the valley, well illuminated despite the late hour, was a huge stone structure in the style of ancient Egypt. A cluster of more modern buildings spread down the valley from it.

Alex shook his head and exclaimed, "This is crazy! There's no valley here. Google Maps just showed a cluster of old farm buildings."

Jen's eyes lit up. "I can see why it's called the Pharaoh Club. Their version of the temple of Abu Simbel is more complete than the original. The two obelisks and full-sized reproduction of the Sphinx are nice touches as well."

When both Alex and Rose turned to stare at her, Jen shrugged and said, "So maybe I was obsessed with Egyptology in middle school."

The road ran the length of the valley, and they followed it through manicured gardens, tennis courts, golf greens, and swimming pools until it reached a grand loop that ran in front of the faux Egyptian temple and its towering Pharaonic statues. They stopped at the foot of the sandstone stairs leading to a towering bronze door. The large gold plaque next to the door was visible from the driveway.

Pharaoh Club
North American access established 1814

CHAPTER 13

Whispers in the Night

I t was two in the morning, and Detective Ramos was sitting in the dark
in his miniscule apartment. He hadn't slept for over twenty-four hours.
Trying to sleep was impossible, his mind cluttered with his upcoming
divorce, the "dead" woman in the dumpster, the security footage from
the hospital, and this afternoon's crime scene strewn with blood and
dismembered human remains.

Ramos didn't need to be a detective to know what had torn those
people apart. Had it been following the missing woman? He would bet
his career on that. She was the key to all this.

The Forensics team had assured him the remains were of two men,
so he was hopeful she'd evaded her pursuer. Even if Ramos did find her,
though, what could she say to him that would make sense?

Ramos's cell phone chimed to life, playing "Music Box Dancer," his
daughter's ring-tone. Two a.m. calls were never good. He snatched up
the phone, cold dread settling in his chest.

"Honey, what's wrong?"

For three agonizing seconds, the phone was silent. Then he heard
the faint sound of Maria's sobbing.

"Mari!"

A cultured male voice responded, "Detective, we have your daughter.
Come to the I-280 Father Serra rest stop. If you aren't there—alone—
within two hours, all that you will find will be your daughter's remains. I
pray, for your sake, that you know what happened to the key the woman
in the dumpster had."

He heard Maria's frightened voice say, "Daddy!"

Then the call ended.

Ramos hands began shaking so badly he dropped his phone. He choked back a sob as he reached down and managed to get a grip on his phone. He called work and waited for someone to pick up. He tried to sound calm but his voice shook, "This is Detective Ramos. I've had a family emergency and won't be in for at least the next week." He hung up before the person on the line could respond.

CHAPTER 14

Mr. Hamad

Rose self-consciously adjusted her borrowed clothes as they walked up to the main door of the club. A doorman with curly blond hair and wearing pseudo-Egyptian garb bowed. "Welcome to the Pharaoh Club." He turned his attention to Rose. "It is an honor to have you here."

The expression on his boyish face hovered somewhere between admiration and stark terror. Rose nodded politely to the man, wondering why he kept staring at her.

The threesome, with Jen holding a squirming Boozer, passed through the open door into a palatial atrium. All attempts to keep an Egyptian theme were lost in here. The walls were covered in gold-veined marble, with matching ornamental pillars, a mezzanine above with a gilded balustrade, and most impressive, a staggering variety of oil paintings, tapestries, displays of gold and gemstone jewelry, and sculptures of all kinds.

Alex stood gazing around him. "Is this a club or a museum? Someone is certainly rich."

Jen appeared to be quietly admiring the beautiful surroundings. Even Boozer calmed down and stopped struggling.

Rose was strangely indifferent to the scene. She felt that she'd seen this many times before. She knew everything was real, original, some of the marble statuary thousands of years old. She knew that the collection was meant to show off the wealth and prestige of the club's owner.

Hearing a discreet cough behind them, they all spun around. An attractive woman with a cinnamon complexion, long ebony hair, and a well-tailored business suit was standing nearby, watching them with dark, thoughtful eyes.

"Welcome, Archivist. I am Chandra Patel. Mr. Hamad is waiting to see you. Your guests and pet are welcome to wait in the lounge. Any food or drink they'd like is courtesy of the club, of course."

"Of course," Rose answered as if she actually knew the rules of the club.

"Will you be okay?" Jen asked as she plucked Rose's sleeve.

Alex was silent, but Rose could see concern on his face as well. She felt a lump in her throat and realized how much she appreciated their concern. She made an effort to sound confident. "You two enjoy yourselves. I'll be fine."

The woman led the group to an open pair of doors at the far end of the atrium. Beyond was a spacious, dimly lit room with tables and booths, each softly lit by a candle. In the center of the lounge was well-appointed circular bar. A number of people sat eating, drinking, and having hushed conversations.

Rose called back over her shoulder as she began following the departing woman, "You two watch yourselves as well."

Rose and Chandra set off down carpeted halls hung with yet more priceless paintings and tapestries, ancient vases and marble statuary expertly illuminated in alcoves. Rose became aware of the increasing warmth as they turned down one hallway after another. She had a sense of déjà vu but could grasp no actual memories. Mechanically matching Chandra's pace, she lost track of how far they'd walked. She was snapped back to her surroundings when Chandra came to a stop. Apparently, they had arrived.

Chandra stood in front of an expensive-looking hardwood door like the many others they'd passed. She inserted a shiny brass key into the lock and turned it with a click. The door swung open on its own, and Chandra stood to the side waiting for Rose. Beyond was only darkness.

Rose gathered up her courage and strode through, not wanting to seem timid. When she stopped just inside the doorway, trying to see anything in the gloom, the door closed behind her.

"Oh Goddess, wonderful," she muttered to herself. In the pitch black she felt a moment of extreme vertigo and almost fell over. Then the lights returned, and she found herself in a spacious office with bookcases, reading chairs, and at the center of it all a huge desk with a distinguished-looking man seated behind it.

"Archivist, I had become concerned. Did you accomplish what you set out to do?" The anxiety in his voice both reassured her and set off her internal alarms.

To break the tension, she said, "Is there any reason it's so hot here? I'm about to get heat stroke."

He rose from behind his desk and smoothed his silk suit. He was a trim, well-dressed man of Northern Arabic descent. His dark hair was graying at the temples, and his features were pleasing to the eyes. His gaze unsettled Rose, though, being both inquisitive and somehow alien. He smiled, but rather than put her at ease, it set her more on edge.

His gaze pinned her to the spot, his voice hypnotic. "Make yourself comfortable, Archivist. Have a seat."

The air grew heavy, and she felt she was going to be crushed by its weight. She realized the sensation was coming from the man.

She didn't move, resisting the urge to sit down with every fiber of her being. "You have me at a disadvantage. My memory is failing me. I am only here because of what one of the men who was trying to kill me said." She felt sweat running down her cheeks as she continued to fight him.

His expression of mock dismay brimmed with just the right measure of sorrow, worry, and relief. "It is well you found your way back here. The task you began must be completed. If you have not already guessed, I am Mr. Hamad."

A brief flash of annoyance flitted across his face before he looked away from her. The crushing weight lifted, and she took a deep breath to remind herself she was still alive.

Hamad opened one of the desk drawers, rummaging around before lifting a bundle out of it. "These belong to you, Archivist. You left them with me for … safekeeping."

He set her things down on the desk.

"Mine?"

Her first unasked question was why she would have left anything here. She approached the desk slowly, her eyes fixed on the two items, making a point not to look at Hamad. One was a well-used, black leather duster that she guessed would hang nearly to her ankles. It seemed familiar and gave her a small measure of comfort. The other object was a large, metal-bound book with a heavy clasp holding it shut, like a manuscript monks might have penned in a medieval scriptorium.

"You are the Archivist," Hamad said, his voice now merely cultured and otherwise unremarkable, "the latest of a long line of women who trace their origins back twenty thousand years to the time of the hegemony of the Atlani people, known today as Atlanteans. You are the keeper and protector of a great store of ancient knowledge."

He touched the book. "Within is the accumulated lore of two hundred centuries. Only with your key can you access it, but I see you no longer have it with you."

Rose put the coat on and immediately felt more in control. "As for this elusive 'key,' it apparently was lost during my trip to the hospital. What exactly does this key look like anyway, so I won't accidentally toss it in the trash?"

Hamad cocked his head and smiled at what was apparently a private joke. "It is an amulet, passed down from the first Archivist. It is the only way to access the book. Within the book are the means to uncovering all the answers you seek."

She buttoned up the leather duster. "I just need to peek inside this twenty-thousand-year-old book from Atlantis? Exactly what enlightenment will I receive if I get this glorified paperweight open?"

He returned to his chair behind the desk and considered her. "You must locate an object. With it, you can foil the plans of the Keeper of Shadows and the entity he is trying to release upon this world. If you fail, the Twilight Veil will tear permanently asunder." He stopped and looked at her.

Rose finally sat down across from him, tired of standing. If she had to play twenty questions again, she could at least be comfortable.

"You know, Mr. Hamad, assuming that you're not just some sleazy con man and that I *am* some creepy librarian from an Atlantean book club, could we just cut to the chase? Why is the pale man trying to tear open this Twilight Veil? How do I find this amulet so I can open this damned book? Oh, and most importantly, why should I give a rat's ass about any of this?"

If she was expecting to get a rise from Hamad, she was disappointed. His face was impassive as he considered her. "Very well, I shall answer what questions I can."

CHAPTER 15

Francis Monroe

Francis Monroe tried to get comfortable in his recliner, but tonight the steel splinters in his back and hip from Afghanistan were letting him know they were there.

He had learned to live with the pain, the wartime memories, and the limited mobility after he'd returned home. Before he had headed off to war, he had married Kate, the cute brunette he'd first met at the local diner. They'd had a son, Alexander. In retrospect he regretted going off to play soldier in the Middle East, leaving his family behind while he went off to prove something, to whom he wasn't sure.

Then he was injured, given a medical discharge, and shipped home. He'd been unable to hold a job, barely able to be a husband or father in any meaningful way—and that was before his wife was killed by a drunk driver while driving Alex home from the library. All he'd had left was a son he'd never quite understood, so bookish and effeminate. If not for Alex's friend Jen, he'd have been sure his son was gay.

Despite his difficulties, without Kate he had to make sure Alex got fed, dressed, and off to school each day. It all became his responsibility. He'd done his best, but the loss of Kate had made his existence hollow.

He rubbed his eyes and felt an unpleasant pang of guilt as he remembered his disastrous exchange with Alex just before his son left home for good.

It had been the year Alex graduated from high school. Alex worked as a bagger at the local grocery store, paying a small amount of rent and helping around the house while he decided what to do with his life. On Christmas Eve he'd announced he wanted to spend the holiday with Jen's foster family next door. Francis, stoned on pain medication in his recliner, had let his pent-up disappointment, frustration, and anger loose. The exact words were a blur now, but the gist of what he'd said was still painfully clear: He'd told Alex that trying to abandon his own father on Christmas showed what a pathetic person he really was—the same kind of shit Francis' own father would have said when he was growing up. Then he'd sealed the deal by implying the only reason Kate died was because his son had needed a ride.

Alex hadn't been back for four years. Francis had finally gotten up the nerve to call his son's cell phone to invite him home for Thanksgiving. Francis had barely had a chance to say word as Alex raged at him before hanging up. Father of the year, he wasn't.

Francis finally slipped off into an uneasy slumber, drifting into a dream. It wasn't his usual dream, where he was having a family picnic with Kate and Alex. At the end, Kate would always walk away, and he'd wake up in a panic, trying to find her, tears in his eyes. This dream was new.

He was in a small, austere flat in London. Only the moonlight shining through a picture window illuminated the bedroom he was in. He was making love to a raven-haired woman named Rose. They had known each other for two years now. She was a bookshop owner, and he was a journalist. Their courtship had been a whirlwind of rides through the countryside on her motorcycle, romantic picnics, attending high-brow plays, and getting lost in intellectual conversations that went on for hours.

His hands lovingly explored her pale, supple body. She studied him with her startling blue eyes as she straddled his hips and rode his erection with loving skill. In the throes of their passion she leaned forward and whispered, "Please don't go, Edwin Prescott. Stay with me, and we can make love until this war goes away." She used his full name when she was serious.

He groaned as he fought to control his rising passion, shaking his head. "I can't put myself before Britain. I'm sorry, but I have to do my part."

A look of sadness crossed her face. She leaned forward and kissed him hungrily as he climaxed.

His moment of ecstatic release faded, and he found himself on a muddy road in Italy near a city called Anzio, a steady rain drenching him and his fellow infantrymen. Several destroyed German vehicles sat on the side of the road to his right. He realized Rose was with him as well. She wore the attire of a male war correspondent, her dark hair cut short to complete the illusion. How she had the pulled strings necessary to be attached to his unit, "male" war correspondent or not, was beyond him. He wanted to protest, tell her to get away from the danger, but before he could, the staccato of German machine guns interrupted him. A hail of bullets tore into the British soldiers, and the scene turned into bloody chaos.

He took cover behind a burnt-out German Panzer IV. The tank had most likely been destroyed by artillery or an air strike, and its dead driver was hanging halfway out of an open hatch, burnt alive. He stared at the dead man's sightless eyes. How long he was transfixed, he couldn't say.

Then he realized Rose wasn't with him. He frantically peered around the tank and saw her, still in the road slogging through the mud. She signaled sharply for him to stay where he was. Then a burst of bullets tore into her back and neck. He watched her blood spray to the earth along with the rain, her limp body crumpling.

He rushed from the cover, staggering through the mud toward her. He realized she was dead, the jagged wound in her neck no longer gushing blood, but that didn't matter. As he neared her body he was stopped short by several staggering blows. At first he felt no pain, but then burning agony exploded in his chest and stomach. He fell down yards from her and struggled to drag himself to Rose's side as he bled to death. He couldn't. His strength had left him, and as his vision darkened, he regretted with all his heart not staying in London with her.

Then he saw Rose above him, holding him in her arms, trying to wipe the mud and blood from his face as she wept. He thought maybe he had died and was with her again, but the hope dispersed when he realized they were still in the mud and rain. The terrible wound in her neck was gone, and only a bit of residual blood and redness showed that she'd been hit.

She continued crying, stroking his cheek as he smiled up at her. Then the dream faded to black, only the sound of her sobbing remaining ...

The ringing phone tore Francis from his sleep. His cheeks were covered with tears. Rose's face was still clear in his mind. He fumbled for the phone and picked it up, sleep still muddling his senses. "Yes, Monroe residence. What is it?"

He was surprised when he heard Jen Sinclair's voice. "Mr. Monroe? Alex has had an accident and needs somewhere safe to rest. Could we and some friends stay at your house for a couple of days?"

CHAPTER 16

The Rest Stop

S till inside his black sedan, Detective Ramos scanned the rest stop from his parking space. Both the parking lot and the two nearby cinderblock buildings were well lit.

There were two other cars in the lot, an old VW van and a gray station wagon. The larger building contained the restrooms, and he noted an older woman moving urgently to it from the station wagon. A man he assumed was her husband followed at a less frantic pace. The smaller building was probably the office for whatever state workers maintained the facility. Along one corner of the larger building was a row of vending machines. No sign of Maria though.

It was 3:15 in the morning, so he'd made it within the time limit. Ramos was shaking and took a moment to get a hold of himself before he exited the car and moved toward the vending machines. He wanted Maria's captor to see that he had arrived.

He stood with his hands shoved into the pockets of his long wool coat. His hand was touching the piece of jewelry that Maria's kidnapper was after. Now he finally understood the years of his wife's anxiety, night after night, that he wouldn't come home. Now he was forced to face the same fear about Maria.

He glanced from side to side as he walked to the vending machines. He put his money in the machine and chose a small bag of trail mix. When his selection dropped down he bent to get it, slipping the medallion from his pocket and dropping it at his feet. He kicked it under the vending machine, out of sight of any casual observer. He wasn't exactly sure why he'd done it, but he needed an edge.

He put the bag of trail mix in his pocket and walked back to his sedan, his eyes taking in every detail around him. He leaned against the front grill of his car, growing anxious at the lack of activity. The elderly couple shuffled back across the lot, climbed into their station wagon, and accelerated onto the highway.

Then the men from the hospital security video were standing in an empty parking space fifty feet from him. He wasn't sure where they'd come from, but the larger man had Maria slung over his shoulder.

This was his first clear view of the smaller man, an impeccably dressed albino whose long hair was fluttering in the cold breeze. He wore overly large sunglasses despite it being night. "Detective Ramos, I am Master Kessler. Do you have the key, or must Yuri hurt your daughter until you decide to produce it?" His voice was civil enough but also somehow lifeless.

Ramos looked around to see if anyone else was near but saw no one. "I'll tell you where the amulet is as soon as I have Maria."

The albino tilted his head and smiled. "I think not, Detective. I care little about your offspring, but until I am given what I want, she is the only bargaining chip I possess."

Ramos drew his pistol, keeping it pointed toward the ground but within plain sight. "I need to know she's not dead."

Kessler's lip twitched, and then he motioned to the big man. Yuri stepped forward to a point half-way between them and dumped Maria on the ground. As soon as the big man turned away, Ramos rushed to Maria's side and rolled her onto her back. She was limp, her eyes open but rolled up white. He pressed his fingers against her neck and felt a weak pulse. When he pulled his hand away he saw blood on his fingers. He realized one side of her neck was smeared with blood.

He looked up at the two men in shock. "What did you do to her?"

Kessler's only reaction was to adjust his glasses before answering. "She's alive. That was what I promised. Now, the key."

Ramos was suddenly pointing his gun at them. "You lousy sons of bitches, you hurt my girl! *You hurt her!*"

Maria moaned, and her eyes closed. "Why did he bite me, Daddy?"

Ramos tried to process the question. Bite her?

Kessler's sharp voice interrupted him. "Now, Detective! I grow weary of waiting."

It took all his effort not to empty his gun into the two men. His reply was an angry whisper. "It's being brought by my partner. He should be here shortly." Perhaps his anger would conceal the lie.

"Yuri!"

The big man stepped forward and scooped up Maria again, slinging her over his shoulder like a sack. Ramos tried to stop him, but Yuri grabbed the front of his coat and threw him through the air. He landed on the hood of his car, the impact knocking the wind out of him.

Kessler's mouth twisted into a frightening smile. "Ten minutes, Detective. That's all your partner has before Yuri begins the slow process of killing your daughter."

CHAPTER 17

The Opal Door

Jen and Alex sat at the bar, eating nachos as they sipped their drinks and watched the surreal clientele in the lounge. Most of the people were dressed in period clothes a century or more out of date.

Jen bent over to Alex. "Is this some sort of Dickens' fair? Maybe a costume party?"

Alex shrugged. "I suppose it could be a belated Halloween party. They're dressed a lot like the guy who asked for directions at the library."

A throaty purr interrupted their conversation. "Is this your familiar? He's adorable!"

Boozer let out a pleased *yip* and jumped from Jen's lap to limp around the new arrival's ankles. The speaker was an Asian woman wearing a red traditional Chinese silk dress trimmed with gold.

She slid up next to Alex at the bar, her body nearly touching his. "You're new faces around here. I am Madame Li, headmistress of the Shan-Chai Academy. From whom are you learning the Art, young ones?"

Alex appeared annoyed and shifted so she wasn't so close. Jen attempted to remain civil as she asked, "The Art? Familiar? I'm sorry, but I'm not sure what you're talking about. We're just waiting for a friend."

Madame Li did not answer, taking Alex's half-finished Mountain Dew and draining the remainder in a single gulp.

Alex flinched and stared wide-eyed at the woman when she ran her hand up his thigh.

Jen grabbed the woman's arm and pushed it away from Alex. "Listen Madame Li, go somewhere else. Alex could do a lot better than you!"

Madame Li sneered at Jen, and her eyes flashed a luminous green. "How dare you lay hands upon me! I shall teach you some manners."

The bartender's voice intruded. "Madame Li, these guests are not familiar with the Art. They are here with the *Archivist*."

Jen didn't miss the subtle emphasis or the sudden fear in Madame Li's eyes. She swallowed and smiled woodenly. "My apologies. I did not mean to disturb you." She turned and hurried away.

Alex turned to the bartender. "What was that all about? Why her hasty retreat?"

The bartender shrugged. "She was hoping to glean trade secrets from new guests." He motioned toward the others in the room. "They were all born with the ability to work the Art. It is hereditary. Yet despite their puffed-up chests and grandiose titles, their mastery of the Art is limited. Even the best of them can barely manage to recreate the Archivist's simplest spells."

Alex watched Madame Li walking away. "So are the Archivist and the club's owner friends?"

The bartender leaned forward, lowering his voice, and said, "No. They've always stayed away from each other in the past. A few days ago, she showed up to see Hamad. No one ever saw her leave though. Practitioners of the Art usually use the ley portals at the Pharaoh Club to come and go. Yet here she is again."

"So did something happen between them?" Jen asked. "Would your boss try to hurt her?"

The bartender shrugged. "That doesn't seem like his style, but he is very secretive and mysterious. No one can say what happened."

Jen turned to Alex. "I hope she's all right. What if she disappears again?"

Alex tried to look unconcerned. "It sounds like Rose can take care of herself."

Jen was about to respond when a woman wearing black motorcycle leathers, boots, and a long leather duster sat down next to her at the bar. Jen and Alex both stared at the new arrival until they realized it was Rose.

"Wow, that's a lot of black leather," Jen commented with a smile.

Rose shrugged. "Long, headache-inducing story. I had this duster waiting for me here. It provided me the remainder of this outfit, like some sort of mystic vending machine."

Jen was intrigued. "Could I have an apple?"

Rose reached into the folds of the jacket and pulled out a large red apple.

Jen's eyes widened, and she accepted the offered fruit, taking a big bite. She mumbled while chewing the apple. "Wow, delicious."

Alex leaned across Jen, whispering to Rose, "So what happened? What did you find out?"

Rose sighed and looked tired. "The owner of this club, Mr. Hamad, told me some pretty crazy things, but I know he's holding much more back. He's the only one talking though, so I'll have to run with what he was willing to part with."

A glance at the other patrons in the lounge revealed they were either looking away from Rose or watching with fright. Rose ignored it all. She reached into her duster and produced an immense metal-bound leather book, with a sizable latch holding the covers shut. When she set on the bar it made loud thump.

"Apparently I'm the keeper of this book, the latest of a long line of people called the archivists."

Jen scrutinized the duster and then the book. "So you're some sort of librarian?"

Rose shrugged and continued with resignation, "That's what Hamad told me, though I suppose there are worst things to be. To open this particular book, I need a key. It's an amulet of some sort and currently in the possession of the police."

Alex ventured, "So why not just go to the police and ask for it back?"

Rose began tapping her fingers on the bar. "According to Hamad, the Pharaoh Club has a mystical door that will take me to 'where I need to go.'"

"A ley portal?" Jen asked.

Rose looked at her, clearly surprised. "I think that's what he called it. Apparently there are ley lines crisscrossing the globe. They're veins of eldritch energy that can be tapped and used to translocate if one has the knowledge or can find an anchor point."

Jen ventured, "So the ley portals are anchor points?"

Rose nodded with a smile. "Very good, Jen. Before we head off, I must reiterate that you three don't need to come along. You can just head home and forget all this nonsense. Who knows what we'll find once we leave the club."

Jen rolled her eyes at the idea of not going. Alex shrugged and tilted his head toward Jen. Boozer just panted and drooled on Alex's shoe.

Rose looked relieved. "Let's go find out how much of this is true then, shall we? Apparently the name of the ley portal we're looking for is the Opal Door."

Rose hopped to her feet and waited a moment for Jen, Alex, and Boozer to join her.

"What about my car," Jen asked as she tried to keep up with Rose.

Rose called back over her shoulder, "Assuming this works, we should be able to return here with little problem."

They left the lounge and headed down one of the hallways leading from the club's main atrium. Jen noted each door they passed looked the same as the last, varnished hardwood. As she followed Rose, the feeling of being trapped in a confusing maze became more and more pronounced. While it seemed like hours had passed, Jen knew that it could only have been minutes. Rose suddenly hung a right down a short hallway that led into a small sitting room with leather furniture, a fancy chess board set up in the center of the room on a low table, and a bookcase filled with what appeared to be identical leather-bound books. Rose wandered along the shelves, examining the books as she went.

Jen was close behind her and saw that the titles, embossed in golden letters, could only be discerned within a few steps of the shelves.

"Um, Rose, there's no door in here. Did we make a wrong turn, or are you just looking for something to read on the trip," Alex asked snidely, but Rose remained focused on her task.

Rose finally pointed at one of the books, examining the gold lettering. "This is it, the Opal Door."

Alex looked confused, but Jen's eyes widened. "So the doorway is the book itself?"

Rose gave her an approving smile. "Pick up Boozer, take hold of my coat, and we'll be on our way. Let's just hope I remember how to do this."

Jen called Boozer over and scooped up the excited, wiggling dog. Once she had a firm grip, she and Alex grabbed the edge of Rose's duster. Rose closed her eyes, then touched the book.

At first nothing happened. Boozer let out a quizzical yip.

Suddenly Jen felt as if they were being swept away by a roaring river, her vision filled with crackling blue fire.

CHAPTER 18

IX Legion Hispana

The ley line's energy coursed through Rose with unexpected intensity, and her mind filled with images that came at her in a jumbled rush. In the time it took her to blink her eyes, she experienced another lifetime as real as any waking reality.

The smell of the unwashed bodies of the Roman legionaries rushing around her made her nose crinkle. She blinked as the smoke from their abandoned fires stung her eyes and the biting cold of the Pictlands made her nose run. Then there was the weight of the dead horse on her painfully broken leg and the screaming, sword-wielding men rushing toward her, wearing little more than dirt and ornate tattoos.

Her poor horse had been killed by a volley of Pict javelins now protruding from its side. She was astonished that she had not sensed the approach of such a huge force of barbarians and was certain now that the wild men had a worker of the Art with them who had obscured their approach.

She turned her attention back to the dead horse lying on her, trying futilely to twist herself free as the sounds of battle surrounded her: screams, the clash of metal, dying horses, and dying men. Luckily the Picts were ignoring her for the moment.

Then a pair of strong hands seized her under the arms as a thick, sinewy leg braced against the horse's carcass. With one mighty pull she was yanked free and fell unceremoniously on her ass, her leg bursting into renewed agony. Her Germanic was poor, but she thanked Hrothgar in his native tongue anyway, her teeth clenched in pain. He hauled her to her feet, and despite the desperate situation around them, she took a moment to glance at her rough-faced lover and smile. She had known him through many lifetimes, but no matter what he looked like, he was always her soul mate.

She reached into her long, hooded traveling cloak and drew one of her swords from within its folds, the dragon-bone grip firmly in her hand.

The Roman legatus legionis had insisted on starting construction of a defensive encampment when they had reached the cairn earlier in the day. She had been unable to begin her investigation of the immense mound, actually more like a hill than any burial site she'd ever seen. The answers she sought were here.

She had pulled strings and called in favors all the way up to the imperial throne to have the IX Legion Hispana transferred to Britannia, serving as her unwitting escorts into the Pictlands under the pretense of a punitive expedition. The realization that the Ancient she had tried to find for centuries might now be before her filled her with an excitement she could barely contain.

She screamed in Latin above the din of battle, "We need to get nearer to the cairn, Hrothgar! Maybe we can get help from the one I came to find!"

Hrothgar nodded his shaggy blond head and began carving a path through the intervening Picts with his heavy iron broadsword. She stood back to back with him, watching their rear as she hopped on one leg to keep up with Hrothgar's advance. Three Picts charged her, and she met them with a deadly series of strikes with her silver sword. She was so quick and precise that the three startled men dropped to the ground in bloody splatters without having touched her with their clumsy attacks.

The cairn lay at the intersection of a web of ley lines, and the ground pulsated with their power. She concentrated, clenching her empty hand into a fist as she channeled the magical energy and called up sheets of pale blue flame that incinerated any Pict it touched. Even the Romans backed away from her and her companion as they moved doggedly toward their goal.

By the time they reached their destination, neither Pict nor Roman would come near them. She looked up at the immense cairn that was as long as three Roman war galleys, covered with dirt, rock, and tenacious plants. She could feel the power of the slumbering presence beneath the cairn but couldn't discern its exact nature. Whatever lay here had slumbered thousands of years. She needed to contact it, stir it from its sleep. When Hrothgar had gotten them within a javelin throw of the cairn, she stopped him with a touch.

With a flourish of her hand, she engulfed another group of Picts in a wave of blue flame to stoke their fear before turning to Hrothgar. "Watch my back, and buy me some time. I must … commune with the spirits."

Hrothgar nodded and smiled at her, long ago having conquered his distaste for her Art. She smiled in return and then faced the cairn, losing herself in concentration. Manipulating the rivers of mystical energy that converged here required her full attention. Any slip in the subtle rechanneling of the power could have disastrous effects for her and the surrounding countryside. Her body became wreathed in flickering blue flame that didn't burn her. She bit her lower lip, and her skin beaded with sweat. She was dimly aware of Hrothgar bellowing out battle cries, the clash of iron and steel weapons, and the screams of Picts and Romans alike who were futilely trying to stop her.

Then she felt the sleeping presence begin to stir. She continued to divert the flow of magic, making sure whatever was there would fully awaken.

She was only vaguely aware of the first tremor that shook the ground. As quickly and safely as she could, she withdrew her awareness from the ley lines and returned to the battlefield. The fighting had stopped when the ground shook, and everyone stood in shocked silence watching the dust rise from the huge mound.

The second tremor was stronger, knocking some combatants off their feet. The Picts furthest from the cairn turned and fled. Others, both Pict and Roman, fell to their knees and beseeched their gods to protect them.

She sensed the Ancient's awakening a moment before it happened. Hrothgar grasped her in his arms, interposing his body between her and the cairn. The cairn exploded in a deafening shockwave that hurled dirt, jagged rocks, and uprooted trees across the battlefield with incredible force. She was thrown through the air, Hrothgar somehow keeping his grip on her. They hit the ground with a jarring impact, her broken leg painfully reminding her of its presence. Hrothgar's heavy body had landed on her. When she finally gathered her wits, she realized Hrothgar's spirit had departed.

She painfully crawled out from under him and looked down at his dead, empty face, and her heart quietly broke. It could be generations before she was with him again. She silently cursed herself for coming here, oath be damned. Around her the Picts and Romans were silent, their bodies strewn about like broken dolls.

"When I began my slumber, the Atlani were fleeing this world, and yet one of their number remains. I look around me, seeing only naked savages and men in shells of metal who claim to be the pinnacle of civilization. What task keeps you here? Why have you interrupted my slumber?" The voice rumbled around and through her, and she suddenly remembered why she was here. She turned toward the cairn.

With a shock she realized the immense mound had actually *been* the Ancient, covered with eons of accumulated detritus and carefully placed offerings. It took her a moment to comprehend the immense creature before her. It spread its vast leathern wings and blotted out the sun. A shimmering hide of metallic scales hissed as it shifted its bulk, and the earth trembled each time its long, lashing tail struck the ground.

She swallowed heavily and quickly slid her sword back into the folds of her cloak, hoping the Ancient hadn't noticed the dragon-bone grip. She stood as straight as she could with her broken leg and fought to suppress the primal terror the Ancient's presence awoke in her. She managed to say in a steady voice, "I am the Archivist and have sought you out since the Twilight Veil descended to protect this world. You must return to where you took form and trouble this world no longer."

The Ancient's immense reptilian head was horned and frilled, but its golden eyes were filled with forgotten wisdom and danger. It was silent for a moment, and she felt a gathering storm. "I prefer this world to the realm of spirits. The Art is all but forgotten here, and the mystical energies have grown potent. I relish the perpetual feast."

She knew forcing him back beyond the Veil might be nigh impossible. She tried to sound brave as she declared, "We remaining Atlani are tasked with guiding and preparing the human race. Your presence stands in the way of our oath. Do not make me force you to depart."

The Ancient laughed, the ground shaking with his humor. "I sense we are evenly matched, Archivist. You may succeed, and again, you may not. Perhaps we can come to other arrangements that would benefit us both …"

With a jarring shock, Rose and her companions found themselves elsewhere. Rose was standing at the edge of a parking lot, two brightly lit vending machines in front of her dispelling the early morning darkness. Jen was several yards away, stumbling and bracing herself against a cinderblock wall. Alex, who had appeared the farthest away, was out in the parking lot. He fell to his knees and began to throw up.

While Rose felt slightly dizzy, she realized she'd ridden the ley lines many times before. Her vision was still vivid in her mind, and she fought to remember what she and the Ancient had agreed to, but it was not there. She had more immediate concerns to deal with in any case.

CHAPTER 19

Battle at the Junipero Serra Rest Stop

R amos struggled to catch his breath, sliding off the hood of his car and landing painfully on the asphalt. For a moment, he thought he was hallucinating. He saw the "dead woman" from the hospital standing across the parking lot near the vending machines. No one had been there a moment before. A thin, red-haired woman appeared near the entrance of the restrooms, staggered several steps, and then braced herself against the wall. A gangly young man appeared mere feet from Kessler and the big man. He immediately fell onto his knees and began puking.

The tall woman glanced around her and took in the scene across the parking lot. She turned and bent down, retrieving the amulet he'd hidden beneath the machine. Ramos's heart sank. He feared she would leave as suddenly as she'd appeared. She had what she wanted. Why stay?

Then the woman shouted above the blustering wind, "Are you looking for this?"

Kessler and Yuri both turned, now in profile to Ramos, and focused their attention on the woman they'd pursued from the hospital. She was holding up the necklace like bait.

Kessler adjusted his wrap-around shades. "I see you've arrived, Archivist, and you've brought friends." Kessler stepped forward and snatched the retching young man by the throat. "Your taste in companions is, as always, questionable. Perhaps we can finally resolve some unfortunate misunderstandings and clear the air."

He motioned to the big man behind him, who dropped Maria unceremoniously onto the ground.

The woman who was apparently called 'the Archivist' began to walk steadily toward Maria's kidnappers, keeping the jewelry in front of her as she closed the distance between them.

"Stop where you are, or I'll snap the boy's neck."

She stopped.

Kessler turned his attention toward the struggling young man. "Let's see what your friend has to tell me, Archivist." He lifted his shades and gazed into young man's eyes.

The tall woman broke into a run, yelling, "Stop!"

The young man's eyes grew wide, and then a horrible, high-pitched scream escaped him. Kessler lowered his shades and dropped his captive to the ground.

"It would seem you really don't remember who you are. Even as an amnesiac, you are a difficult woman to track down. I knew the police would lead me to you if I was patient."

Ramos watched the exchange, hoping against hope that he and his daughter might survive this. He retrieved his pistol from the ground even though he knew it would do little good against these two. He had to get Maria when the chance presented itself.

The Archivist had stopped her advance when Kessler dropped the screaming young man. Her voice was clear and level. "Well, here I am. What do you and your pet want?"

Kessler's lips twitched, and the big man growled deep in his chest. The albino forced a smile as he replied. "Address me as Master Kessler. Even amnesia is no excuse for such a lack of professionalism to one above your station."

The Archivist laughed. "Above my station? The only thing you and the walking meat slab seem to be masters of is incompetence. He tries to kill me and fails. You slink around following the police to find me because you're too inept to do it yourself. I'm only professional with those who aren't buffoons."

At this point the big man growled, his lower jaw distending and unhinging like a snake's. His gaping mouth bristled with jagged, slavering fangs.

Ramos wanted to scream and could see from the Archivist's face that she was tempted to do the same. To her credit, she held her ground. "Does he fetch balls and roll over too? I'm not just going to give you this. We could let bygones be bygones and go our separate ways. That way you can take mastiff-boy home to give him his Alpo."

Kessler finally gave up his forced pleasantries, and his face had become a dour white mask. "Since you are here, my need for the key is irrelevant. I want to know the location of the Tsaritsyn artifact. I know Hamad returned your book to you, and now the policeman has managed to restore your key. Just give me the information, and I'll be on my way."

The big man's features had become more bestial as Kessler spoke, his mouth stretching far wider than it should have been able to, his hands twisting into huge, hairy paws with black talons.

The tall woman swallowed but betrayed no emotion. "What exactly is the Tsaritsyn artifact?"

Ramos started as a small black animal jumped up onto Kessler's shoulder. He tried to decide what it was, but its glowing red eyes seemed to rule out something from the local pet shop.

"The information would be in your book. Given your inherent stubbornness, I have no delusions that you'll hand over the information willingly. Perhaps I'll have Yuri here try to persuade you?"

He studied her, then shook his head. "No. Your mental and physical toughness are legendary. Perhaps flaying the skin from the broken policeman or his daughter would be more persuasive? Or I could let Yuri inflict his cruelties on your hysterical companion here."

Ramos tensed, not sure what was coming next.

The Archivist had stopped only twenty feet from Kessler and his hulking monster. She showed no overt response to Kessler's threats. He began to speak again when she drew three slender throwing blades from her duster and snapped them at his head in a precise, fluid motion. As the three silver blades embedded deeply in his forehead, Kessler's face was frozen in an expression of complete surprise as he crumpled lifelessly to the ground.

The black creature on his shoulder jumped clear and scuttled under a Volkswagen bus parked nearby.

Yuri roared, dropped to all fours, and charged. He was now an enormous, shaggy thing ripped from someone's worst nightmare.

In the confusion, Ramos ran to Maria and scooped her up, carrying her back to his car. He saw the redheaded woman rush over and drag the screaming young man away from the charging beast.

*****

Rose drew a long silver sword from her duster, just like the one from her dream, the dragon-bone grip pressed reassuringly into her hand. Maybe she shouldn't have thrown the blades, and Kessler's lack of reaction made her think it was something her old self would never have done. The memory of her past was gone though, along with whoever she used to be.

The big man Yuri, or what he'd transformed into, was charging right at her. She hesitated, distracted momentarily by the Grendel's ear-shattering roar. This ruined her plan to bring her blade down on the monster's head. The beast's slavering maw snapped the air where she had been standing as she spun gracefully out of harm's way.

As the monstrous creature barreled past, Rose still managed to deliver a single wicked slash that sliced through flesh and grated against bone. She smiled in satisfaction at its howl of pain and the splatter of blood from its rump. The beast now had four ass cheeks. She hoped she'd given him chronic hemorrhoids as well.

The Grendel didn't slow down, its momentum carrying it into the chain-link fence forming the perimeter of the rest stop. The fence buckled with the monster's thunderous impact, the support posts bending and then snapping as dark blood cascaded from the creature's wounded buttocks. The Grendel continued on, dragging a portion of the destroyed fence with it as it fled across a field and disappeared into a cluster of trees.

Rose caught her breath but stayed alert, not wanting any more surprises. Without thinking she produced a rag and wiped the blood from her sword's blade. Then she somehow stowed both items back in the folds of her duster.

She turned toward the Hispanic policeman and the young woman he was holding protectively. Her two companions were a few feet away. Alex had stopped screaming and was now curled in a fetal position, whimpering. Jen held his head in her lap. Rose guessed the policeman's companion was his daughter. He looked up at Rose, and she saw tears running down his face. "I think she's dying."

Rose knew she could do nothing for Alex. He would have to pull through on his own. She went to the policeman and knelt to gently examine the girl, feeling her temperature, checking her neck, noting the sickly pallor of her skin. Rose didn't take her eyes off the young woman when she spoke to the girl's father. "I'm Rose, by the way."

He blinked back his tears. "Detective Steven Ramos. This is my daughter Maria."

Rose nodded, finishing her exam. "She's been infected by Kessler, but I think there's time. I'm still feeling a pulse."

Rose closed her eyes and, just like in her vision, began gathering the ambient energies from the nearby ley line. She heard Ramos gasp as her hands became wreathed in flickering blue flame. She opened her eyes and moved to take Maria's head in her hands.

Ramos pulled her away defensively. "What the hell are you doing?"

Rose needed to convince the detective of the gravity of the situation. "Listen, I wish I could give you an answer. But, Detective, if you don't let me help her very soon, she will be gone."

She gave a sigh of relief as he let her lay her fire-wreathed hands on Maria's head. Rose closed her eyes again, and her whole body stiffened. She sent the energy she'd gathered into the young woman, letting it burn away her unnatural sickness and injuries.

Rose opened her eyes and saw Maria do the same. The young woman's breathing was steady, and color had returned to her face. Maria smiled weakly up at her.

Jen's frightened voice came from behind Rose. "Where's Kessler?"

CHAPTER 20

Night Terrors

Jen sat next to Alex as he lay in his old bed at his father's house thrashing and talking incoherently in his sleep. They'd reached his dad's just after five in the morning. Other than a series of curt nods and pleasantries, Alex's father had remained silent as Alex had been carried into his room. Jen knew that once morning came, they would all have some explaining to do. She only hoped Alex would be all right.

*****

Alex was drowning in the pools of blood that were the albino's eyes. He was lost in a crimson freefall as Kessler probed the depths of Alex's mind. He could feel his memories being uncovered, scrutinized, and then tossed aside. As he tried to hold onto his sanity, he realized vaguely that Kessler's mind was shared by another; its maddening hunger for blood made Alex choke. Then he found himself somewhere he didn't want to be.

"What am I going to do with you, Alex?"

Alex was eight years old and riding in his mother's SUV. His mother impatiently passed a slow vehicle as she continued in an angry tone. She was usually angry when Alex was with her.

Alex felt small and had to blink back tears. "I was reading. I lost track of the time."

This was all terribly familiar to Alex. He always came here during his worst nightmares.

"You missed your damned bus yet again, and now I'm going have to skip yoga class! Why can't you be a normal kid? No friends except Jen next door, no after-school activities, no sports with the other boys?

Instead you spend a nice day like this in the library with your nose in a book."

Alex's voice was tiny. "I'm sorry, Momma."

"And don't even get me started on what a disappointment you are to your father. He might not say it out loud, but I see it on his face every time you two are in the same room. Alex, at this rate you're never going to amount to anything."

Those were the last words his mother ever said to him.

A black pick-up truck ran the red light and broadsided their SUV so hard it rolled over three times before coming to rest on its roof.

It took Alex a moment to gather his wits. He was upside down, and his broken ribs made it hard to breathe. His mother hung lifelessly from her seatbelt, the side of her ruined head covered in blood.

"Momma? Wake up."

Unlike the countless nightmares before, this time his mother's dead eyes opened. She fixed a hateful gaze on her son. "The world would be better off if you'd never been born!"

Alex began to cry, then scream, as this new part of the nightmare unfolded with a life of its own.

His mother reached up and began peeling the blood-splattered skin from her face in ragged strips. Beneath was gnarled, gray flesh that looked like petrified wood.

Alex tried to stop crying, struggled to undo the seatbelt holding him captive, but it was jammed.

The face beneath his mother's skin was that of an ancient hag. The hideous face smiled, and Alex saw its mouth was filled with rows of sharp metal fangs. The solid black eyes were empty and soulless. Her voice was a soft cackle. "You'll be joining her soon, man-child. Soon you will *all* mourn my coming."

Alex awoke with a strangled scream, soaked in sweat. Jen was there to hold him as he sobbed uncontrollably.

CHAPTER 21

Breakfast at the Monroe Residence

It was almost noon, but Francis had decided breakfast would still be the easiest thing to prepare. His houseguests sat around the kitchen table, enjoying the scrambled eggs and bacon he'd already cooked. Now he was making the traditional family pancakes, with a touch of cinnamon and vanilla, he used to prepare every Saturday morning. That was, before Kate had died.

The policeman, Detective Ramos, was at the head of the table, his daughter Maria to his right. He was drinking his coffee from an oversized mug that read "World's Best Dad."

He still hadn't had a chance to talk to Alex, who was seated next to Jen. He seemed distant, distracted, but kept insisting there was nothing wrong.

Francis felt something leaning against his ankle and looked down at the gimpy pug, Boozer, staring up at him hopefully. There was something comforting about the pug. Boozer's limp made Francis feel like the dog was a kindred spirit. Another wounded veteran of a forgotten conflict.

Then there was Rose. He kept stealing glances at her. Despite her shorter hair and biker leathers, he knew it was the same Rose from his dream, the svelte beauty he'd made love to and died trying to save. Now he was paralyzed with indecision. How could he broach the subject?

Oh, by the way, I had a dream where we were having great sex but ended up getting shot by Nazis.

He wondered if she would even notice given how absorbed she was in reading the ancient leather book lying open before her.

Michael S. Ripley

She'd only waved her hand in acknowledgement when Ramos thanked her for helping his daughter Maria.

The detective addressed his comments to Francis and Maria. "Her hands were covered with blue fire! If I hadn't been so shocked, I would have grabbed Maria and run away. Thank God I didn't."

He turned back to Rose. "*La mierda*! What the hell is going on? Giant boogey men, albino vampires, voodoo magic? None of this crap's in my job description."

Rose stirred from her book and looked up at Ramos. "Wish I could tell you, Detective, but this book isn't what I was hoping for. It's like an index, with references to books that must be elsewhere. Other than some handwritten notes next to the entries, it only offers bits and pieces. However, I have gleaned a few clues."

She paused, staring blankly at a light fixture on the wall. Alex cleared his throat. "Would you deign to share with the rest of us?"

Rose's eyes came back into focus. "Oh yes, where to begin? First, the book has numerous references to the Twilight Veil and the incorporeal beings trying to enter this world from beyond it. Almost all these formless entities need to possess a physical body to exist here. Some of the more powerful, primal spirits have grown strong enough to form their own bodies when they come across."

Francis turned from his frying pan. "So what's this Kessler trying to accomplish? Open a door?"

Rose looked at him. "Apparently so. The Twilight Veil goes through cycles and sometimes grows weaker. It's at these times that something escaping into this world is most likely. Just a few days from now will be one of these times, and Kessler is looking for a talisman to help him bring one of these trapped entities into this world."

Francis watched her as she tried to talk around the eggs into her mouth. She obviously wasn't a fan of Emily Post.

Maria finally spoke. "So what's a talisman?"

Rose straightened in her chair, swallowing a mouthful of eggs before saying, "In this case, it appears to be a human skull. If Kessler acquires it, he may very well succeed in opening the door."

90

Ramos shrugged and gave a clipped laugh. "Isn't he out of the picture? You stuck three knives into his skull."

Rose shook her head. "He'll be back. Once he's recovered he won't let his guard down again. According to a handwritten note here, the skull is somewhere called the 'Dancing Hut.'"

Ramos's eyes widened. "We found you in a dumpster across the street from the place. It's a strip club."

Rose scowled. "I was in a dumpster?"

Francis gave Rose the first batch of pancakes in hopes of lightening her mood. She glanced up at him. "Thank you, Mr. Monroe."

"Please, call me Francis."

She dug into the pancakes even as she was pouring syrup over them. "Wow, Francis, these are delicious!"

Francis watched Rose eat with amusement. She certainly had an appetite. As he served more pancakes, Francis ventured a guess. "So once you're all done eating, someone needs to head over to the Dancing Hut and nab this skull?"

Ramos shrugged. "I'm not going to be able to use my badge to get us far. Don't have any probable cause for a search warrant or any legitimate police business to get in. But I don't want to lose track of Miss Rose again, so I'll go with her."

Rose lifted her fork affirmatively as she chewed her mouthful of pancake.

Francis suddenly felt ashamed. "I wouldn't be much use. Shrapnel is making it so I can barely walk today, let alone go on some adventure at a strip club."

Rose swallowed and examined Francis. "You were a soldier?"

He turned and noticed her attention. He felt giddy and turned back to his skillet. "Yeah, didn't Alex mention it? I was a corporal with the US Army, in Iraq fourteen months before an IED went off near our vehicle. Lucky me, I was the sole survivor."

There was an uneasy silence, Francis at a loss what else to say. How did you explain war to a civilian? You couldn't.

Rose seemed oblivious to the tense quiet. "Francis, I'm having a staggering sense of déjà vu. Have we met before? I feel like I know you from somewhere."

Her expression was so earnest. The dream replayed in his head. "Maybe, a long time ago."

Rose scrutinized him for a few moments and then turned to Ramos. "When do we leave for the club?"

Ramos looked from Rose to Francis and then back again. "The club doesn't open until six."

Rose shook her head. "We need to get there while the sun's still up. Neither Kessler nor his guard beast can function very well until the sun has set."

Francis was crestfallen as Rose stood up, impossibly slid the big book into her leather duster, and turned to the detective. "So let's go. We'll play it by ear once we get there."

CHAPTER 22

Returned in Blood

Yuri stood amongst the towering snow-powdered pines, bundled in a long down jacket and fur-lined boots to keep the cold at bay. It was late at night, and a large bonfire was the only source of light in the dark forest. Yuri guessed they were somewhere in Europe but wasn't exactly sure where. The seven people he'd kidnapped spoke some German-sounding gibberish that he couldn't understand. Despite being shocked when Kibit had begun whispering to him, he'd followed the instructions.

He had stripped, bound, and hung the shivering captives from the trees above the stone slab where Kessler's lifeless form lay. The silver blades that had been imbedded in Kessler's skull had been torn out by Kibit, leaving ragged wounds. Now the small creature scurried from captive to screaming captive, carving intricate symbols into their naked flesh with its small black claws.

Yuri watched the show impassively. He was more concerned with the agonizing, burning ribbon of pain his ass had become since being cut by that librarian bitch's sword.

Normally the monster bound within him could heal injuries almost instantly. However, the cut inflicted by the woman's blade was mending very slowly and still hurt like hell. At least the wound had finally stopped bleeding.

Yuri's attention returned to the scene before him, and he growled in irritation as he watched Kibit work. How he hated the vile creature and the disquiet he felt when it watched him with its tiny red eyes. Even the Grendel stirred nervously under the scrutiny of the creature.

Michael S. Ripley

He pushed thoughts of the grotesque little aberration away and shifted his stance painfully. Instead he contemplated the raven-haired woman who had inflicted this humiliation on him.

Kessler had assured him that this Archivist was of little actual danger, bound as she was by the Atlani Codes. Kessler had been sure she would reveal the location of the artifact he sought, one way or another. Instead she'd handed them their balls on a platter and sent them packing without breaking a sweat. Yuri's faith in Kessler and his supposed power was severely shaken.

Unless she had an identical twin, it was the woman he'd shot. How the hell had she survived three bullets to the back of the head? He'd been told she was just some pretentious librarian, a member of an ancient sorority that guarded knowledge predating the fall of Atlantis. Yeah, right.

Granted, after the ceremony that had bound the spirit of the Grendel within him, he'd become slightly less skeptical of this mystical bullshit.

At the thought of the Grendel, Yuri's blood burned; murder and violence filled his mind. The beast stirred within him, and it took all Yuri's considerable will to hold it in check.

Kessler had been careful not to reveal his plans. However, when he'd removed his glasses and peered into Yuri's eyes, Yuri been forced to relive murdering his own brother when he was twelve. It had been a memory he had suppressed for a very long time. The connection had worked both ways, however, and Yuri had gleaned some facts of his own.

Kessler wanted to rip open a barrier and call *something* into this world. Yuri had nothing but contempt for his fellow humans and couldn't care less what happened to them. He had personal reasons for the disquiet he felt regarding *what* Kessler wanted to summon.

Kessler called her "Grandmother," but Yuri knew her by her Russian name, Baba Yaga.

As a small boy his own grandmother had taken sadistic delight in frightening him with tales of the Russian witch. In her bedtime stories, Baba Yaga flew through the sky in a giant stone mortar that she steered with an oversized pestle. She would devour naughty children with a mouth filled with sharp iron teeth or tear them limb from limb with

94

long, clawed fingers as strong as steel. He was filled with dread at the thought of his childhood nightmare being real.

What bothered Yuri even more was Kessler's reason for doing this in the first place. How much of this plan was Kessler's doing, and how much was arising from … elsewhere?

Yuri's attention was wrenched back to the ceremony as the captives' screams suddenly became more frantic and pain-filled. Kibit finished carving a symbol in Kessler's forehead with a bloody flourish. The matching symbols on the captives' writhing bodies began glowing crimson. Vaporous tendrils of blood burst forth from the symbols and streamed to the glyph on Kessler's forehead. Yuri watched the surreal scene until the screams died down to whimpers and sobbing, then stopped altogether. Bloodless, shriveled husks were all that remained of the captives when the scarlet streams finally stopped flowing. The terrible wounds on Kessler's head had vanished.

The Grendel surged within him, anticipating fresh corpses to feed on. Yuri's stomach turned at the thought, but he knew once the Grendel took over, he would relish the feel of human flesh and bones being crushed between his misshapen teeth.

Kibit hovered near Kessler's body, hopping back and forth impatiently. Yuri started as Kessler sat up, gasping for air. Yuri looked away from the albino's exposed eyes, remembering all too well what he'd seen the first time. The albino fumbled for his nearby shades and slipped them on. He then turned to Yuri, smiling. "Come, we have work to do if we want to be ready for Grandmother's arrival."

CHAPTER 23

Showdown at the Dancing Hut

Rose stood impatiently at the entrance of the alley where she'd been found lifeless in the dumpster. She held Boozer in her arms—the dog had somehow snuck into the detective's car before they'd left.

Ramos stood next to her, watching the people passing on the street—gangbangers, prostitutes, drug addicts, and the homeless. This wasn't one of the better neighborhoods in town. "Shouldn't you leave that thing in the car? God, I hate small dogs. They're like overgrown rats."

Boozer looked over at him in alarm, eyes wide, his contented panting halted.

"He helps me think," Rose said softly while staring at the strip club across the street. Afternoon was waning, and they'd found all the doors to the club locked. "Maybe we can go to the rear door and break in."

Ramos's annoyance was clear. "I'm still a policeman. Without probable cause, there's nothing I can legally do."

Although Rose was watching the front of the club, her gaze seemed far away. "Something's not right here." She shifted her stance, and Boozer let out a small whimper.

Ramos was actually considering her suggestion of breaking and entering when he saw the thin, sickly child that Meyers had tried to chase down the night they'd found Rose in the dumpster. His large, somber eyes were unmistakable. They still gave Ramos a chill. He was watching them from down the block, hugging the corner of a brick building.

"Get over here, kid! You have some questions to answer!"

Ramos turned to Rose. "See that kid? He was …" Ramos turned to point him out, but the child had vanished.

Instead of calling him on the mystery child, she squared her shoulders and handed him the squirming pug. "You wait here with Boozer, and I'll have another look around back," she explained with a sly wink.

Ramos almost tripped over his own feet trying to catch up with her as she jogged quickly across the street. As a law enforcement officer, he wanted to protest her obvious intent to break in. Boozer squirmed, apparently not liking him any more than he liked the dog. By the time he caught up to her at the club's rear delivery door, she was entering the now open doorway.

Boozer twisted, letting out a long yowl, then broke free from Ramos's grasp. Once on the ground, Boozer waddled through the doorway after Rose.

"*Dios maldito*! Boozer! Rose? Get back here," Ramos called out in a harsh whisper. He heard nothing. "If this costs me my retirement," he grumbled.

He entered the darkened storeroom and, after a couple of wrong turns in the dimly lit hallways, found Rose and Boozer in the Dancing Hut's main room. The dirty windows made the sunlight from outside dingy, and the smell was a combination of a filthy public restroom and stale alcohol. The stage was small, with just a single pole for whatever unfortunate dancer worked here. The antique hardwood bar and dusty shelves of liquor behind it took up a lion's share of the space.

Rose was scanning the room. "Well, if we can't find the skull then maybe we can just have a couple of drinks."

Her remark only irritated Ramos. "Just find the fucking skull, and let's get out of here!"

Rose shrugged and turned back to the bar, moving cautiously behind it. The light was murky at best. Ramos stood amongst the tables, each with four chairs stacked on top. He looked down at Boozer, who was rolling around in the filthy sawdust that covered the floor. "Disgusting mutt," Ramos growled. Boozer rolled onto his stomach, sneezed, and began panting.

"Success! Doesn't anyone ever clean around here," Rose muttered, holding up a cobweb- and dust-covered human skull.

Boozer began barking frantically.

"Shut the hell up, you stupid mutt," Ramos snapped, swinging around to glare at the pug.

"Oh *Carajo*."

Two familiar figures and three that were not so familiar stood near the doorway they'd come through earlier. Travers and Garcia, the missing FBI agents, were both leveling government-issue Glock 22s at them. The three remaining men looked like non-descript construction workers carrying crowbars. All of them appeared a little rough around the edges, like they were just getting over a long, serious illness.

"Give us the skull, and you can live," Agent Travers commanded flatly.

Ramos managed to catch Rose's wink as she called out. "Sure, here you go." She hurled the skull across the room. It landed with a thud next to the stripper's pole on the stage.

Ramos had the presence of mind to leap behind one of the nearby tables. Even as he fumbled for his pistol, he saw Rose vault over the bar and land gracefully in a crouch. In her hand was the same silver sword she'd used against the monster at the rest stop.

Agent Garcia ran toward the skull, ignoring everything around him. Travers and two of his cohorts moved to head off Rose. The remaining man came toward Ramos, swinging his crowbar at nothing in particular as he got nearer.

Despite the gloom, Ramos drew a bead on Garcia and opened fire, feeling a sense of satisfaction as he saw the man flinch as at least one of the rounds slammed into his back. Garcia barely slowed down, trying to grope for the skull with one hand while the other continued to hold his firearm.

Rose called to Ramos as she began weaving between the tables toward Travers, "These men are dead! You need to hit them in the head if you want to force out the things possessing them!"

Ramos didn't take time to argue, drawing a bead on Garcia's head just as he lifted the skull triumphantly in one hand. The first shot nicked Garcia's ear while the second struck the back of his head. Garcia took one halting step forward, dropping his prize into the putrid sawdust. An unearthly wail escaped from Garcia, and Ramos squinted and covered his ears at the horrifying sound. With a bright flash, Garcia crumbled into ash, his empty clothing falling into a heap.

Ramos had almost forgotten the man with the crowbar and jumped back just in time to avoid catching a blow against the side of his head. Ramos leveled his gun and shot the man in his right eye. Another terrible wail, and the man crumbled into ash. Ramos thought damned souls in hell must make the same noise.

The crack of Agent Travers' Glock snapped Ramos back to reality. As the two men with crowbars tried to box Rose in, Travers was trying to hit the rolling and spinning Rose, who was kicking furniture at them to add confusion.

Ramos snapped off two shots at one of the crowbar wielders, bracing himself as one of his shots caught the man in the side of the head. The alien, mournful wail raked across his nerves, making him choke.

The second man with a crowbar turned his attention to Ramos, charging toward him with a roar.

Travers continued firing at Rose, and splinters and smoke filled the air until the click of Traver's empty pistol spurred Rose into a final charge. She drove her sword's blade up under his chin, the point exiting the top of Travers' head. An inhuman howl somehow escaped Travers, despite the fact that his mouth was pinned shut.

Ramos didn't have time to react to the sound of Travers' demise, finding he was out of bullets as well. The last assailant barreled toward him. He sprang forward and tackled the man, wrestling the crowbar away from him. He straddled his struggling opponent and brought the crowbar down on his head, again and again. Ramos fell backward in horror as the last wail echoed through the bar and the body crumbled into ash.

When his head cleared, Rose was kneeling beside him, a look of concern on her face. "You going to be all right, Detective?"

He wanted to assure her he was fine, but he only managed a sob as the nightmare screams continued ringing in his ears.

Then the front door of the bar was open, unsullied sunlight blinding Ramos as someone exited with the skull.

Rose hurled her sword like a javelin as she bolted toward the closing door. The sword stuck in the doorframe, wobbling as Rose crashed through the door. All Ramos managed was to struggle to his feet. It was the small, sickly child he'd seen earlier that had absconded with their prize.

Ramos was still standing there on wobbly legs when a winded Rose came back into the bar. Her expression told him they'd lost the skull.

CHAPTER 24

Damage Control

The sun had set outside as Rose paged through her oversized codex at the kitchen table, looking for any tidbit of information that might help find the skull, the child, or, most importantly, where Kessler was taking it. All she'd been able to determine was that the skull was a mystical anchor. It would allow "Grandmother" to enter this world and stay here.

She didn't need an intact memory to know that this was very bad. She'd really screwed up being so flippant, tossing the skull around like a child's ball. Now she had to make things right.

Ramos sat silently across from her, looking both sullen and unnerved. Curled in his lap was a sad looking Boozer, who had wisely fled the bar when the fight had begun.

Alex walked into the kitchen and took in the scene. "You two look cheery. Whose hamster died?"

Rose didn't look up, continuing to page through her endless book. "I got the skull snatched from under our noses. We need to come up with a plan B, which is tricky since I didn't really have a plan A."

Alex offered sarcastically, "Where's my dad? He fancies himself a military tactician. Maybe he could crap out a plan."

Ramos scowled at Alex's tone. "He's resting in his room. His injuries were acting up."

Rose shut the book with a loud slam. "Ramos, could you see if there's some place called Ravenwood around here, or at least some variation of the name? The book keeps alluding to some base of operation, and I finally found a casual mention of the name. While you're doing that, I'll look in on Francis. You're right, Alex, despite your bad attitude. Your dad might be able to help. By the way, where's Jen?"

Alex sat at the kitchen table, obviously biting back a snarky remark. "It's that time of month. She's been in the bathroom."

Rose nodded without really comprehending, got up, and left the kitchen. When she reached the door to her host's room, she knocked softly, waiting until she heard Francis call out, "It's open."

She entered and shut the door behind her. He was lying on the top of his bedding in jeans and a T-shirt. "Heard you weren't feeling well."

He chuckled, started to shift on his bed to face her but stopped abruptly, wincing in pain instead. After a few breathless moments, he muttered, "Damn it. The only thing I have to show for fourteen months in Afghanistan."

Rose sat on the edge of the bed. "You seemed to know me earlier. I could see it on your face. It's not that simple though, is it?"

He closed his eyes and sighed. "You wouldn't believe me if I told you."

Rose shrugged. "I've been fighting oversized hell beasts and trying to steal skulls. I think you'd be surprised what I'll believe at this point."

He closed his eyes and smiled before responding, "Just a dream. We were lovers in London. You looked like you do now, though I was a journalist named Prescott. We both ended up getting shot by Nazis in Italy. Wacky, huh?"

His description sparked a distant but disturbing recollection, and she quickly changed the subject. "I might be able to help you with your injury. With your permission, of course."

"Wait, let me guess. You're some holistic, New Age, crystal-waving healer? Don't bother. I've tried everything." His tone indicated he'd resigned himself to a life of chronic pain long ago.

She pressed gently, "Then what do you have to lose?"

He considered her, sighed, and nodded.

She took his hand firmly and cleared her mind. "Just relax. The worst-case scenario is our hands get sweaty."

He chuckled and let himself sink back onto his bed.

She closed her eyes and called the energy from a hidden place deep inside her. The blue fire burst to life and began to fill her. She could hear the concern in Francis' voice, but it was distant and ethereal. His injuries became clear to her: the steel slivers and damaged muscle, nerves, and bone. This would be much easier than Ramos's daughter. No supernatural element to complicate the healing. The drain on her would be minimal.

She sent the power now filling her into him. She felt him try to pull his hand away, but her grip was too strong. The blue fire filled every fiber of his being and scoured the injuries and pain away. For a moment their spirits touched, and she realized who he was: her soul mate, made manifest in this time and place. The realization shook her to her core.

Francis went limp, sinking into a deep sleep. Rose stumbled to her feet and hurried out of the room as a deluge of fragmented memories assailed her, filled with frightening implications she wasn't ready to face.

She returned to the kitchen in a daze. Alex was throwing a tennis ball to an excited Boozer, and Ramos was still seated at the kitchen table tapping at a laptop. She looked at the wall clock and noted it was nearly seven in the evening. Over an hour had passed.

Ramos looked up at her. "Is everything okay? You look shaky."

Alex just snorted, dropping the ball and leaving an excited Boozer behind.

It took a moment for Ramos's words to make sense. She fought to focus on his face. "Fine. Everything's fine. Francis is sleeping. Anything on Ravenwood?"

He nodded, glancing back at the monitor. "Seems there's a residential high rise a few blocks from downtown San Jose called Ravenwood Tower. Ring a bell?"

Rose stood next to him, looking at the computer screen. "Not really. Maybe I was renting an apartment or working for someone there? Do you have a way to show where it is?"

He clicked until a Google map appeared, showing Silicon Valley and a marker pinpointing where the tower was.

She had sensed a ley line junction a couple of miles away when they'd returned from the Dancing Hut. "I should go and check it out. Once I know what's going on, I'll have something to tell you all."

Ramos laughed. "No way, Miss Rose. I'll be driving you there in my car. Don't think after all the shit we've been through that you're just taking off by yourself."

She didn't want to go alone but wasn't going to endanger these people any longer. "It's been a long day, Detective Ramos. You should get your daughter home. Kessler won't be bothering you or your family any more. He has what he wanted."

Ramos looked like he was going to argue the point, but then he glanced toward the living room where Maria was asleep on the couch. "You're right. Her mom's going to be pissed as it is. But I'll be coming back here, so don't disappear anywhere without telling me first."

She gave a grudging nod. "I promise that once I know what's going on we will meet back here and decide what to do next."

Rose finally realized Alex had left the kitchen. He was obviously upset about something, but Rose was too rattled by her visions to try to find him. She'd talk to him when she got back.

CHAPTER 25

Walk to the Park

Rose had only walked a block through the suburban neighborhood before she realized she was being followed. She let her hand slip into her duster, ready to draw her sword.

"Wait up, Rose," a breathless voice called.

"Goddess, Jen, be careful," she chided as the thin redhead jogged up next to her.

"Can I join you?" Jen was wearing a down jacket and stocking cap that made her look like a skier.

Rose hesitated. "Only as far as the ley junction. After that, it could get dangerous."

Jen smiled. "I could get hit by a bus or have an aneurysm. Just being alive is dangerous."

Rose looked over at her new companion. "How profound. Are you a philosopher in your spare time?"

Jen looked away self-consciously. "Well, I am a bartender. I suppose I've learnt a lot about human nature pouring drinks."

Whatever the reason, Rose was glad that Jen was joining her.

"So Alex mentioned you weren't feeling well. Something about it being that time of month," Rose asked, fearing the worst.

Jen looked at her as if she were expecting a joke to follow the question. "I wish Alex would just keep his mouth shut, but really, you don't know what that means? My period, my monthly cycle, you know, cramps, bleeding—the birds and the bees?"

Now it was time for Rose to feel embarrassed. "I, I guess not. I've forgotten so many things."

Jen softened her voice. "Have you ever had children?"

Rose answered without thinking, "I can't have children." Where that had come from, she didn't know. She knew it was true though.

Jen looked sad. "I'm sorry."

Rose felt uncomfortable with Jen's sympathy. "So what about Alex? He seemed upset when I left. Any idea what that's all about?"

Jen gave a half smile. "He tends to see the worst in everyone and everything. He's always been too sensitive for his own good. He jumps to ludicrous conclusions with few or no facts. We were neighbors and friends since we were both five years old so I know how he thinks."

Rose tried to figure out what could have set Alex off and then laughed. "I was in his father's room for nearly an hour. I bet he thinks Francis and I were having sexual relations."

Jen shrugged. "That wouldn't surprise me. Not sure why he should care who his father screws, err, has sexual relations with. Alex and his dad aren't on the best of terms. He hasn't talked to his father for nearly four years."

Rose chuckled. "Not much of a romantic, are you?"

Jen hugged herself. "I'm twenty-two, and the only guy I've ever had sex with is Alex. Our romantic relationship barely lasted one night."

Rose realized she'd broached a topic she'd rather not explore. She wondered if putting her fingers in her ears and humming loudly would be rude.

Jen continued, apparently not noticing Rose's pained expression, "My biological parents were drug addicts. My little brother Danny and I were little more than inconvenient mistakes. More often than not, we went to bed hungry—no birthdays, no holidays. When I was five, Danny got sick, a flu that became pneumonia. My parents wouldn't or couldn't do anything. So I called 911, and before I knew it, Child Protective Services had separated me from my parents and brother."

Rose hesitantly put a hand on Jen's shoulder. "I'm so sorry."

Jen turned and smiled in gratitude.

"When my foster family, the Sinclairs, took me in, Alex was my neighbor. He was too small, too smart, too sensitive, the constant victim of bullies. I guess he became my chance to make up for failing my brother.

We became friends, and I became his self-appointed protector as we grew up."

Jen paused, and Rose felt the need to say something. "That's admirable."

Jen looked embarrassed. "We decided after our senior prom that we would become lovers. After all the years we'd known each other, it seemed like the right thing to do. We rented a hotel room and went to it. What can I say? It was both magical and forgettable, full of clumsiness and emotional turmoil. Early that next morning we both just decided that we felt like we were sleeping with our sibling. That, as they say, ended that."

Rose wasn't sure what to say or if she should even care. "So why do you and Alex live together? Seems like it would be difficult."

Jen was looking off into the distance. "I guess I feel like I still have to protect him. I should move on with my life, but I'm afraid to leave him alone."

Rose slid her arm around Jen. After a moment, Jen put her arm around Rose's waist. "Thanks for listening, Rose."

Rose was quiet for a time. "Well, sorry I couldn't be of more help. Maybe if I get my memory back, I'll have loads of useless advice to give you."

Jen laughed. They finished their walk in silence. When they reached the small park where several ley lines crossed, Rose turned and placed her hands on Jen's shoulders. "We're here, Jen. I'm off into uncharted territory. Why don't you head back and have a conversation with Alex about what you both want for your futures. I'll be back as soon as I can, and you can let me know how it went."

Jen looked into Rose's eyes for an awkwardly long moment, a curious expression playing across her freckled face. She took one of Rose's hands and squeezed it, then turned and walked back the way they'd come.

Rose watched Jen until she was out of sight. She figured she hadn't botched that too badly. Maybe there was hope for her rebuilding her interpersonal skills after all.

She turned and focused, tapping into the invisible energies crackling around her, and in a flare of pale blue fire she was on her way.

CHAPTER 26

Ravenwood Tower

D owntown San Jose was a flurry of evening activity. Rose skulked out of the abandoned lot she'd appeared in and joined the stream of college kids and couples out for dinner, shopping, or bar hopping. She felt as alone as she had when she was a homeless person just a couple days ago. Granted, a part of her preferred being left alone, invisible to the rest of the world, but a part of her yearned to join into conversations, find out who people were, where they were from, what their lives were all about. As much as she wished to be included, though, she knew she would always be on the outside, looking in.

Getting her bearings was trickier than she'd expected. The name Ravenwood Tower meant nothing to those she asked. Luckily the address was not as cryptic, and after zigzagging through twelve blocks of stores, boutiques, restaurants, hotels, and residential neighborhoods, she reached East Santa Clara Street and Tenth. On one corner of the intersection was a twelve-story high rise made mainly of tinted black glass and steel. It seemed out of place yet completely inconspicuous as well. The foot traffic was not nearly as heavy this far from the downtown corridor, and she made her way to the main doors of the building without passing anyone. The windows and glass doors were tinted, but Rose could still make out a lit lobby inside.

"Archivist." A voice interrupted her reconnaissance. It was Chandra Patel, Hamad's assistant from the Pharaoh Club. Rose watched her close the distance between them, trying to get a read on the situation. Why was Hamad's assistant here of all places?

Rose didn't realize she was in danger until Chandra was next to her. A long knife appeared in the woman's hand and was thrust toward

Rose's stomach. Rose had no time to think, managing to pivot away just enough to raise her hand between her midsection and the knife thrust. The blade pierced her hand, the protruding crimson blade coming just shy of her navel. Rose used her free hand to grab Chandra's knife arm and twist it until she released the weapon. With a shove, she toppled Chandra backward onto the pavement.

Rose cried out in pain as she pulled the knife out of her hand. Blood dripped freely onto the sidewalk from the ragged wound. "Goddess, that hurts! What is wrong with you? Are you insane?"

Chandra swallowed nervously and, despite lying on the ground, managed to square her shoulders and answer firmly, "Hamad wanted me to delay you. You're moving more quickly than he would like."

Rose was impressed by the woman's chutzpa. She leaned the knife against the curb and broke the blade with her boot. She picked up the pieces and tossed them onto Chandra.

"Tell Hamad to come do his own dirty work next time. I'm sick of dealing with underlings."

Rose reached into her duster and brought out several white cloth bandages that she wrapped around her injured hand. When she'd put enough layers on that the blood finally stopped soaking through, she took a deep breath and pushed Ravenwood Tower's main door.

It wouldn't budge.

She felt like an idiot as her would-be assassin watched her antics blankly from the ground.

An electronic buzz startled her. It continued until she pushed the door again, and this time it opened. She rushed through the doorway, afraid it would slam shut if she dallied. When she glanced back through the window, Chandra was gone.

The lobby was cold, spacious, and constructed of gloomy black marble, a number of potted ferns giving the only splash of color. Behind a security desk next to the elevator was a plump, elderly man in a doorman's coat and hat.

Rose tried to act like she belonged here, striding confidently up to the desk. As she reached her destination, she had no idea what to say. She was thankful when the man spoke first, his voice both officious and faintly nervous. "Hello, Miss Ravenwood. Should I let Reginald know you're on your way up?"

She glanced at his name tag and smiled. "Hello, Lester. How are things going?" If she'd slapped him across the face, he couldn't have looked more shocked.

Rose pressed on despite his silence. "No, no. Let me surprise dear Reginald. By the way, Lester, a quick test—what's my first name?"

Despite the oddness of the question, Lester managed to respond, "Your first name? It's, Alysia, ma'am."

He pushed an unseen button behind his desk, and the elevator doors opened with a faint *ding*.

He cautiously inquired, "Will you be needing anything else, ma'am?"

She smiled. "Nothing else. Have a nice evening, Lester." She walked over and entered the elevator. She turned to face the lobby and noted Lester staring at her with a stunned expression as the elevator doors closed.

Rose felt a little sick. Alysia Ravenwood? Given his reaction, she must have been a particularly unpleasant person. She found herself liking Rose much better or maybe even Monique.

The elevator lurched into motion. According to the digital numbers flashing on the readout above, the elevator finally stopped on the top floor. The doors slid open, and Rose found herself in a black marble landing, as cold and gloomy as the lobby. There was a single, ornate walnut door across from the elevator. She walked cautiously across the atrium and stopped, seeing the door was decorated with carvings of mythical creatures—dragons, griffons, werewolves, faeries, sea monsters, vampires, and mermaids—intertwined artfully.

As she raised her uninjured hand to knock, the door swung open. Rose peered into the dark hallway beyond but saw no one. She called out loudly, "Hello!"

No one answered.

Rose stepped through the threshold and descended a short flight of stairs that led into a hallway, leaving the door open behind her in case she had to run. As she reached the end of the hall, the door slammed shut. She sighed in resignation and entered a sizable, well-appointed reading room. Packed bookcases stood against the walls, and overstuffed chairs and sofas were arranged tastefully, with reading lamps strategically placed. There were halls leading deeper into the apartment off to her right and left.

Rose ran her uninjured hand reverently over the leather furniture and then perused one of the bookcases. The books looked old and were in a variety of languages: Old English, Spanish, Greek, German, Italian, Russian, and ancient Persian from a cursory glance. The titles indicated that the books dealt predominantly with history and philosophy.

She went down the short hallway to her left. When she reached the end, she saw open doorways to either side, one revealing a dining room and the other a gleaming, modern kitchen.

Rose stepped into the kitchen and almost fell over backward as a tall, severe-looking man in a charcoal-gray suit stepped silently into her path.

"I see you've decided to return, Miss Ravenwood. I am beside myself with giddy delight. I take it your planned arrangement with the Keeper of Shadows fell through?" His English accent and sarcasm were both laid on thick.

This wasn't what Rose had been expecting. "You must be Reginald?"

Reginald sniffed. "Really, ma'am. Who else were you expecting? No, let me guess. You planned a wild party, and the guests were supposed to be here already, awaiting their beloved hostess as they drank your expensive wine and sampled delicious appetizers prepared by yours truly?"

Rose wasn't sure how to react to his steady stream of derision. "Are we a couple or something?"

His stony expression broke into a smile, and he laughed. "It's hard to catch me off guard, ma'am, but that was very amusing."

She relaxed slightly. "Thank you, but honestly, do I work for you as a maid or something?"

A burst of laughter erupted from the man. "Oh, stop it, Miss Ravenwood! A maid? You and cleanliness are mortal enemies."

He turned away and walked over to an ornate coffee machine, flipping a switch to start it, still chuckling to himself. "Some coffee for you, ma'am?"

Rose closed her eyes and exhaled. Enough of this verbal sparring. "Reginald, I woke up in the hospital, my memory's a wreck. I can't remember this place or you, so humor me for a moment. Who am I, how are you connected to me, and what is this place?"

Reginald considered her as if she might be joking again. When she didn't speak, a look of concern touched his features. "I do believe you're serious, ma'am."

She pulled her injured hand from her pocket. "And also, someone just stabbed me in the hand. Do you have a first aid kit I could use?"

He strode over and, with a light touch, guided her into the dining room. He gently but firmly sat her in one of the chairs at the table. "The injury to your hand will heal itself shortly. As to who I am, call me your assistant. I take care of the mundane matters of everyday life while you fulfill your duties as the Archivist."

Reginald crouched and looked into her eyes like a doctor, cocking his head in puzzlement when he'd finished. "You currently go by the name Alysia Ravenwood. You own this building, along with thirty-eight similar buildings around the globe. I would have to check our records to tell you exactly how many lesser properties you own; coastal villas, warehouses, European mansions, antique and rare book stores, et cetera, et cetera. What do you know about the injury that put you in the hospital?"

Rose stared at him, waiting for a punch line. "You're kidding, right?"

Reginald pressed. "Your head injury, Miss Ravenwood. Tell me about it."

She shrugged. "I woke up with an agonizing headache, bandages swaddling my skull, nausea, confusion, sensitivity to bright light. Detective Ramos probably knows more about the details."

Reginald stood and examined the back of her head. "Still faint scarring on your scalp. This is all wrong. And who is this Detective Ramos?"

The question made Rose feel like she'd broken some unspoken rule. "He and several other kind people have gotten me this far. Friends, I suppose."

Reginald's eyes widened ever so slightly. "Friends? Obviously something must be very wrong. Contact them and arrange to meet them somewhere nearby. I need a chance to speak with them."

Rose frowned. "Why not just have them come here?"

It took Reginald a moment to respond. "This is one of your sanctums. Having outsiders here is unprecedented!"

Rose felt terribly weary. "Well, time to set a new precedent. I'll call Ramos and Francis to let them know. Can you arrange to have them picked up?"

"Of course, Archivist. As you wish," he answered officiously. "I must say, ma'am, I'm glad you have returned home."

Rose thought the statement had some profound, unspoken meaning but was too tired to care. "After I call them, I'm going to rest Reginald. Wake me when they get here."

CHAPTER 27

Volgograd (formerly known as Tsaritsyn)

Colonel Anton Popov barked an order at the milling throng of soldiers, his voice echoing in the cavernous aircraft hangar. Despite the utter strangeness of the situation, the Spetsnaz unit fell into formation, adjusting their special gear with practiced precision. The remainder of his force would be made up of regular army units from the Volgograd garrison.

The blizzard had sprung to life without warning two days ago and continued to increase in strength and area. The howling winds were deafening, and the snow flurries now limited visibility to only a few meters. Popov's orders were to take the hastily assembled strike force into the forests east of Volgograd and reconnoiter the area. Initial satellite photos indicated it was there that the weather anomaly had begun. None of their intelligence gathering systems were able to reveal more than this.

General Orlov stepped forward to give the elite platoon of men the briefing Popov had already heard. Despite his rank, Orlov was a bureaucrat. He was well versed in navigating the corridors of power at the Kremlin but lacked any actual field experience. Popov had misgivings about him being in command of this operation but remained silent. He'd rather remain an army colonel than a forgotten prisoner in some Siberian labor camp.

The general's briefing was short and to the point. He finished by wishing the men good luck, and Popov realized Orlov wouldn't be coming along on the mission. He was relieved.

Popov stepped forward, and at his order, the platoon piled into the four BMP-3 infantry fighting vehicles in the hangar. As soon as the hatches were sealed, the engines roared to life, filling the hangar with diesel smoke.

As Colonel Popov and his Spetsnaz troops set out into the snowstorm, their convoy was joined by vehicles leaving the other aircraft hangars along the flight line: an infantry company in eleven BMP-2s and a company of twelve T-80 main battle tanks with an additional platoon of three of the newer T-90s alongside. Given the extremely limited visibility on the ground, GPS satellites would guide them to their target location.

It took over five hours to cover just fifty-two kilometers in the blizzard. As their convoy had struggled through the snow-choked landscape, Popov felt a growing disquiet. It was a primal, invisible terror that made his skin crawl.

There was no question when they reached their destination. The blizzard suddenly stopped, left behind as they entered a large forest clearing that was calm and devoid of any snow. Popov gave the order to dismount over the radio, and when the hatches opened, he joined his three hundred plus soldiers as they assembled outside. He did a quick head count and realized they'd lost two of the BMP-2s and a T-80 somewhere in blizzard. The remaining tanks pulled forward of the dismounted troops and formed a firing line. He pulled out his binoculars and scanned the wide clearing. His men and the tank crews waited for him to give orders.

The scene before him was confusing. At the center of the clearing was a ghostly circular fence made of bones, topped with human skulls. Within the enclosed yard was an equally insubstantial log hut complete with a peaked, thatched roof. The specter of an old, stooped woman wearing a peasant's dress, a shawl, and a head scarf was in the yard as well, looking like countless other Russian babushkas. She took measured steps around what he mistook for a cauldron. When she took a gray stone pestle as big as an oar and began grinding something inside, he realized it was a great stone mortar. Popov's blood ran cold as he caught a glimpse of the woman's face and realized the shriveled hag was something other than human. With growing panic, he turned to his radioman, who stood at the ready next to him. His order came out as a high-pitched scream. "All units target the structure directly ahead! Fire at will!"

His radio operator relayed his order.

The tanks opened fire, the deafening crack of their 125 mm guns drowning out every other sound. The infantrymen took up firing positions between the tanks with their machine guns and assault rifles and opened fire as well.

The rain of destruction continued for several minutes until Popov motioned to his radioman to relay a cease-fire command. As an eerie silence descended, the distant howl of the blizzard was all that could be heard.

The smoke hung so heavily across the clearing that, even with his binoculars, Popov couldn't see anything for several frustrating moments. When the smoke cleared sufficiently, he saw only cratered ground surrounded the hut and fence. Neither had suffered any damage. Then his men were crying out, panic in their voices. Popov lowered his binoculars and followed their terrified gazes upward. Hovering above them, much closer than the distant hut, was the ghostly, ancient woman. She sat floating in her huge stone mortar, the oversized stone pestle in one hand and a broom in the other.

"Impossible," Popov whispered. The bedtime stories of his childhood rushed back upon him—horrid tales to keep children well behaved, threatening them with the wrath of the cannibal witch, Baba Yaga, if they were bad.

Popov could see her face clearly now, an impossibly ancient hag with a hooked nose and black eyes. She smiled, revealing a mouth filled with glinting metal fangs. Her silence as she considered them threatened to drive Popov mad, but her rasping voice speaking a dead Slavic dialect they could still understand only made the reality infinitely worse. "Rude, unpleasant men and their toys. Some things never change. I will teach you manners, even if it kills you."

Popov grabbed the handset from the radioman and screamed, "Retreat! Back into the blizzard!"

The ancient witch set her broom down. Her long fingers wove glowing runes in the air as the soldiers tried to run, fall back to the relative safety of the blizzard and the trees. Popov felt the spark of hope in him go dark as immense, misshapen trees burst from the ground of the peaceful clearing between his force and the snow-shrouded forest beyond. Some of his men opened fire while others began screaming in fear. The trees lurched forward, tearing themselves from the ground. Their thick, oily roots and writhing, knotted branches began entangling and crushing every soul in their path.

The ground erupted beneath the tanks and BMPs. Green vines as thick as a man's leg braided themselves around the vehicles, through their road wheels, and in between their metal tracks. Popov and several Spetsnaz troopers saw an opening in the chaos at the same time and made a break for the blizzard.

The sounds of tortured metal and snapping steel drowned out the screams of the soldiers. The vehicles were destroyed: gun barrels were bent, road wheels broken off, and tracks torn apart as the vines did their work.

As his men were slaughtered behind him, Popov and his five companions passed through the terminus between the clearing and the blizzard. The sounds from behind were mercifully faint as the howling wind filled his ears. He and his surviving men lost themselves in the frozen forest.

CHAPTER 28

The Council Meeting

Reginald examined the black tooth that the surgeon had removed from the wound in Rose's head at the hospital. It was etched with a number of barely perceptible runes that were now glowing.

"Well, Reginald, any insights?" Rose asked anxiously from her seat at the head of the dining room table. Francis, Alex, Jen, Boozer, and Detective Ramos watched from their own seats.

Reginald set the tooth down in front of Rose and sniffed. "All I can say for certain is that it's a dragon's tooth. A master of the Art has woven enchantments into it, but as to their nature, that is your specialty, ma'am, not mine."

Reginald retreated to the kitchen and returned with a silver tray with cups of coffee and tea for Rose's guests.

"We're still no closer to finding Kessler or the skull. We need to find out where he's taking it," Rose said as much to herself as the others.

Detective Ramos fidgeted with an unlit cigarette that Reginald had made clear he was not to smoke in the apartment. He tapped it on the table. "Don't any of you watch the news?"

Alex snorted. "We've been a little busy, Detective, in case you hadn't noticed."

Ramos ignored Alex. "My ex had the news on when I took Maria home. While she was hollering at me, I was watching the television. Eastern Russia. A storm no one can explain that is growing. You said that he's trying to bring a Russian witch into the world?"

Rose pondered the information for a moment. "Kessler asked me for the location of the Tsaritsyn artifact. Tsaritsyn. It was the old name of modern-day Volgograd, which was Stalingrad during the Soviet Union's Great Patriotic War. That's where I need to go to put an end to all this."

Reginald set a cup of coffee down in front of Rose. "Ma'am, you need rest. To be blunt, you look like shit."

Rose laughed. "I am having trouble seeing straight." She pushed the coffee away. "And I definitely don't need caffeine. Reginald, make our guests comfortable. Once I've gotten some rest, I'll take them home and do what I have to."

A cacophony of protests arose from around the table, but Rose lifted a hand and silenced them. "I need rest. We can have a discussion once I'm up, but it will end with you all going home and me taking care of this task in Russia."

Rose stood up, making a point of not meeting anyone's gaze. Boozer, sitting in Jen's lap, had his head on the table trying to sniff the dragon tooth. Rose snatched the accursed thing, handed it to Reginald, and left the dining room. Francis, no longer hobbled by his wartime injury, went after her. The others only exchanged worried glances.

"Rose, wait," Francis called out as she reached the door Reginald had identified as leading to her bedroom. She opened the door but hesitated on the threshold.

His voice was hushed, filled with excitement. "You saw it all, too, when you healed me. We were meant to be together—we are soul mates. I know you saw it."

She closed her eyes and gestured for him to follow as she entered her bedroom. As soon as she shut the door, he embraced and kissed her. She didn't pull away but didn't respond either. She could feel his desperate arousal through his pants.

He stepped away from her. "What's wrong?"

She tried to look at his confused, hurt face but instead ended up looking down at her boots. "This is too much, Francis. Too many unexplained memories swirling in my head. Most of them not really memories so much as images of someone else's life, someone I don't know."

Francis loosened his grip but still held her. "It must be reincarnation! We return to be with each other again and again."

Rose looked up at him, fear and anger in her voice. "Then why don't I ever change in the memories, in the images? Why do I always look the same in these past lives, both mine and yours?"

He hesitated.

She took a deep breath. "If you want to stay with me here, you need to do something about your pent-up sexual energy. Go in the bathroom and … relieve yourself."

Francis looked incredulous. "But I want to be with you."

She turned her back on him and started to undress. "I'm not ready. If you really believe we're soul mates, then power down your libido."

As she folded her leather duster on the bed, she heard him retreat into the bathroom and shut the door.

She thought she heard a faint moan at one point, but otherwise Francis was silent. She finished undressing, putting her folded clothes on the dresser, and then slid under the covers. When Francis finally returned, flushed and out of breath, she murmured, "You can join me."

He looked at her folded clothes and began undressing himself. She watched him as he undressed, some small part of her wanting to make love with him, but her wounded mind hushed any desire she had. He set a large knife on the dresser alongside his clothes.

"What is that?" she asked, trying to divert herself from her turbulent thoughts and emotions.

His expression became wistful. "My dad gave it to me when I was a kid. A survival knife with a compass, fishing line in the handle, the works. The only good memory I have of him was when he gave it to me on my tenth birthday. Now that I can walk without pain, I decided to start wearing it again."

He finished undressing and slid into bed next to her, spooning her from behind. She pulled his arm around her and set his hand on her stomach. "Just hold me, Francis, while I sleep, and I'll try to believe we are soul mates as well."

As she lay there, her eyes half closed, he gently caressed her. The slow, gentle touch of his hand was the last thing she felt as she drifted off to sleep.

CHAPTER 29

A Very Important Appointment

The hulking Russian military transport had all-wheel drive, but even so, Yuri fought to control it as they drove through the blizzard on what had been the main highway running out of Volgograd. Kessler sat in the passenger seat, wrapped in blankets despite his layers of cold-weather clothing. He was lost in thought. Kibit sat up in his lap, its black fur rippling and red eyes peering through the windshield with anticipation.

Yuri had remained silent since they'd ridden the ley line into Russia. His disquiet had only grown as he became more certain that he was taking part in something that would lead to his own destruction. For the moment, he was still free of the Grendel, so he shouted to be heard above the howling blizzard, "Is zis vat you really vant, Master Kessler? Vat do you have to gain from bringing her into zis world?"

For a moment, Yuri thought that Kessler hadn't heard him or was ignoring him. Yuri had to strain to hear as Kessler spoke. "I am weary, Yuri. She promised to set me free from the crushing weight of the millennium. That is all I wish for any longer. I had hoped the Archivist would join me, but it was not meant to be."

Yuri didn't feel any more confident after Kessler's answer. "And rest of us? Vat vill happen to rest of us?"

Kessler smiled. "Humankind no longer deserves to be protected. Why would the Atlani wish to return to a world with such hateful, selfish creatures? They prey on each other like starved animals, allow the world to be polluted in their greed and apathy, and cling to their tribal mentalities like sheep. Grandmother is their creation, Yuri, so let them have a good, long look in the mirror."

125

Michael S. Ripley

The vehicle lurched, and Yuri fought to keep it from sliding off the highway. "Vat vill she do?"

Kessler stroked Kibit's fur before answering. "She was born of men's cruelty, hate, and injustice against the innocent, especially women. Her ire was kindled by sadistic hypocrites who validated their atrocities by branding their victims with names like witch and warlock. Everything she does here will be in direct response to mankind's own heartlessness."

Yuri said nothing else. He could feel the weight of the skull in the satchel he was wearing and began pondering what it was that he wanted.

CHAPTER 30

Dreams of the Atlani

Rose dreamt and found herself in the library of her mind once again. The books on the shelves were neatly arranged, the floor clear of debris, the post-apocalyptic ambiance of her first visit gone. She walked through the well-ordered aisles of books to the center area where the silver caretaker, Ayesha, sat at one of the many large tables.

The raven-haired angel considered her sadly. "Archivist, I have repaired what damage I could. I regret to inform you there is one portion of your mind that I am unable to restore."

The awe and caution of her first visit was gone, and Rose simply sat at the table across from Ayesha. "Pray, do tell."

Ayesha sighed in annoyance. "Archivist, this is serious. Your knowledge of the Art, of the great archive, is intact, but who you were and are, those memories have been extinguished from your mind. All your experiences, the things that defined you as an individual, are gone."

Rose thought she should have felt more distraught or emotional about this news but found herself strangely indifferent. "Is this a normal occurrence?"

A single tear fell from Ayesha's silver eyes. "No, it is not normal. This was the result of the tooth placed in your wound after you were injured. The Keeper of Shadows had hoped you would join him, so it is unlikely he did this. You were suffering as much as he after all the long centuries and wanted it to end."

The rising dread that Rose had felt for some time now came to a head. "Please, tell me how old I am."

Ayesha stood, her wings of light unfurling around her. "I had hoped you would remember, that I would be spared trying to explain, but fate has decided. Using today's system of dating, you were born in 18545 BCE. Your people were the Atlani, a civilization that had already existed over five thousand years before you were born, and—"

Rose interrupted. "Atlantis? Are you saying I was born in *Atlantis?*"

Ayesha nodded. "The Atlani civilization owed their longevity to their mastery of the sciences of dimensional architecture and physics. Simply put, they had discovered countless other dimensions. They'd learned how to open doors to these dimensions, travel to them, conquer them for wealth and slaves, and most importantly, how to tap the limitless energy of these dimensions, to power both Atlani technology and their ability to do magic."

Rose let Ayesha's words sink in, feeling overwhelmed as she did so. Ancient civilizations, other dimensions, magic, angelic storytellers—she wanted to disbelieve it all but knew deep down it was true. She was scared by the terrified despair rising inside her.

Ayesha's voice became darker. "Then disaster struck. A new dimension was discovered. A thousand Atlani scientists, soldiers, and explorers went through the door they had opened. A moment later they returned, missing half their number. Almost all who had returned were insane, but this wasn't immediately apparent. They had entered a dimension where physical form was unknown. It was a place of spirit, mental energy, entities that were sensitive to thoughts and memories. The Atlani who had been ejected from this dimension had all been possessed by these formless spirits. These entities could not exist in this world without a physical form and were using their Atlani hosts to do some exploration of their own."

Rose interjected, trying to distract herself from her own anguish, "The Twilight Veil. That has something to do with this dimensional mumbo jumbo, doesn't it?"

Ayesha sighed and nodded. "But you are jumping ahead. The full magnitude of the disaster was only realized when the possessed Atlani began to physically change. The beings from this alien dimension reveled in their new physical forms and began to embrace Atlani fears, beliefs, myths, and emotions. Nightmares took form, mythic monsters became real, and the Atlani realized it was only a matter of time before they were destroyed by what they had let loose upon their world."

Ayesha paused, but Rose didn't interrupt, grappling with her own inner turmoil. "So the greatest scientists and workers of the Art devised a plan to both seal away the encroaching dimension and escape the ravages of those creatures that remained in this world. It was determined that ten specially chosen Atlani, the greatest practitioners of their particular fields, would stay behind to maintain the protective veil and destroy or return the remaining invaders to their own dimension. Once it was safe for the Atlani civilization to return from the dimension they'd fled to, those who had remained would open the way."

None of what was being said awakened any memories for Rose. "So ten Atlani were picked to stay behind. How were they able to live as long as you claim?"

Ayesha blinked. "These ten were bound to spirits from a myriad of other dimensions so they could carry out their duties without interruption, without aging and dying. You were one of those ten, Archivist. You were a great Atlani general, with a mind disciplined and strong enough to become the repository of all Atlani's knowledge and history. You became the Archivist."

Rose felt overwhelmed. "Where are the other Atlani? Why aren't they dealing with this crisis as well?"

"Only you and the Keeper of Shadows remain," Ayesha said, sounding sad. "The other eight have fallen to misfortunes their bound spirits could not save them from. I am the spirit that was bound to you, Archivist. I have kept you young and whole for all these twenty millennium as you have fulfilled your oath and kept the Twilight Veil intact."

Rose was angry now, not only at the tale but at herself. "Who in their right mind would agree to this, to an endless existence? How could anyone be such a short-sighted fool?"

Ayesha regarded her. "For you, General of the Black Rose, patriotism; a sense duty honed by your military background; a wish to preserve your civilization; and, most importantly, your Atlani arrogance. I cannot read your thoughts or follow your reasoning, but I've watched, listened, stood alongside you through the ages. There was no hesitation for you when the time came to accept this mantle."

Rose's shoulders sagged as she processed Ayesha's words. That wasn't who she was anymore. How would she go on? Did it even matter? She bit her lip and then met Ayesha's eyes. "What must I do?"

CHAPTER 31

From Russia, with Hate

F rancis was at a loss as to why Rose wouldn't allow him to come with her. "You can't go alone. This has to be a team effort. Can't you see that?"

Alex muttered just loud enough for his father to hear, "After last night, maybe she doesn't need a fuck buddy anymore."

Francis turned on Alex. "What did you say, you self-centered ass? Just because you've gone through rough times doesn't give you license to be a disrespectful punk. Everyone goes through rough times. Grow up, Alex—that's fucking life!"

Alex laughed caustically. "Is that your fatherly wisdom? You know what I think about 'fucking life'? In the end, everyone will throw you on the trash heap of their life—friends, family, soul mates. Look at you, for example. You knock up Mom, then leave to go play soldier. When you come back, you can barely walk. Mom has to take care of you while you lay around because of an injury you never needed to suffer, which gives her an excuse to ignore me even more than while you were gone. Then Mom goes and dies, leaving you in the lurch, and you reluctantly raise your disappointment of a son. At least in the end you told me how you really felt. Then four years pass before you intrude and take what little I have. You steal Rose away from me, continue to treat me like I killed Mom with my own hands, and I'm supposed to give a shit about your philosophy of life? If not for Jen, I would have stepped in front of a fucking train a long time ago."

Francis was silent, suddenly at a loss for words. He felt like Alex was a stranger he was seeing for the first time. When he answered, it was with a touch of sadness in his voice. "I'm sorry I didn't live up to your expectations, son, but I did the best I could. If you wanted perfection, I was the last person you should have looked to."

Rose stepped between them. "Great Goddess, I don't *belong* to anyone, Alex—not to you or your father! I'm not a pet! If you want to know what happened last night, *ask Francis!* Now, no more discussions, no more bickering. I'll get you all back within walking distance of the Monroe residence, then go do what I need to do in Russia. I'm the Archivist, not any of you. You go home, be adults, communicate, and try to be a family."

Despite the stunned silence all around, Ramos spoke up. "What if you fail, Rose? At least if we go with you, we'll all have tried. What am I supposed to tell Maria if I hide here while the world ends?"

Boozer waddled up and leaned against Rose's leg, looking up at her with a lolling tongue.

Rose was suddenly shouting, tears in her eyes, "Damn it, this is hard enough! I can't drag you all into danger, I can't be responsible for your deaths." She covered her face with her hands. "You're the only friends I have."

Jen walked over and put an arm around Rose's shaking shoulders, her voice trying to convey levity. "Can't you at least take Reginald? You barely know him at all."

Reginald interjected, "Unfortunately I am unable to travel via the ley line network. My means of transport would have to be more mundane."

Jen sighed. "I was kidding, Reginald. It was a joke."

Rose gently removed Jen's arm and, blinking back tears, said in a tone that brooked no more arguments, "Join hands, form a circle. Time is short."

Francis grabbed Rose's hand. "This isn't over, Rose."

Rose didn't look at him. "It will be when you get home." She focused, and suddenly they were all plunged in a raging river of pale blue fire, tossed and spun like leaves in a hurricane.

*****

Biting cold, howling wind—those were the first things Francis was aware of. He opened his eyes and peered into the dim light of the forest. It was either twilight or perhaps night with a bright moon trying to pierce the clouds of the snowstorm. Windswept snow stung his face. He shielded his eyes and could barely make out Alex and Ramos sprawled in a snowdrift nearby. Ice-shrouded trees surrounded them. Francis struggled to his feet, his California autumn garb doing almost nothing against the cold.

Francis shouted at the others, "Get up! You need to move, or you'll freeze!" The others struggled to their feet.

Ramos stood and shielded his eyes. "Where the hell are we? In LA we fucking complain if it's fifty degrees. This is bullshit!"

Francis tried to get his bearings. "I'm guessing Eastern Russia. Something must have gone wrong with Rose's spell."

Alex was shivering. "What do we do?"

A part of Francis appreciated his son actually asking him for advice. Survival was their first concern. Francis pulled out his smart phone and found it powered on but didn't display anything but static. He unsheathed the survival knife his father had given him and, using what little light his phone gave, checked the small compass in the handle. Let's head north. I looked at maps of the area before we left, and the main highway in the region runs west to east. From this terrain, it looks like we're to the south of the road. Let's just hope I'm right about where we are."

They fell in behind Francis as he led them through the forest, setting a brisk pace to keep them as warm as possible. Thankfully the trees blocked the worst effects of the wind so their long march didn't end with them freezing.

Their trek was mercifully short. Francis finally stopped, pointing ahead. "There, through the trees. It looks like a road." Alex and Ramos were tired, so he helped them forward. Indeed, despite the thick layer of snow, they exited the woods onto a wide road. The main evidence of it being a highway was the presence of snow-spattered freeway signs nearby.

As they walked onto the road, the snow reached their knees. Francis realized this was going to be slow going; with the freezing storm, they'd probably be dead before they made it a half a mile.

Then Ramos shouted above the tortured wind, "Headlights! A vehicle is coming!"

Francis followed the detective's gaze, and sure enough, headlights in the distance were getting closer. Francis thought it must be a military vehicle, able to negotiate the snow with its headlights still visible.

He wondered who they were but didn't have to consider his options long to come to a decision. He began waving his arms over his head to get the driver's attention. Ramos and Alex followed his lead.

*****

"Jen. Jen, wake up."

Jen slowly gained consciousness, murmuring, "Why's it so cold?"

When she opened her eyes, she realized the blizzard might have something to do with it. Boozer was licking her face, and Rose was kneeling next to her, a look of relief on her pallid face.

"Thank the Goddess you're all right. Something went wrong. The energy in the ley lines is being disrupted by the breach in the Veil. Whether I like it or not, we're both in Russia now, and the others probably are too."

Jen sat up and realized she had a thick, fur-lined coat on, its hood pulled over her head. Rose slipped matching mittens on her hands. As Jen stood, Rose produced a similar winter coat from the folds of her duster and slipped it on, pulling the hood up over her head. "Goddess, I hate the cold."

Jen thought they looked like stereotypical Eskimos. "Where do we go, Rose? Do you know the way?"

Rose closed her eyes and focused. "Yes, I sense the source of the storm and the mystical disruption. I can sense the Grendel as well. Follow me."

Jen scooped up a shivering Boozer, tucking him inside her jacket. The dim light and driving snow made it hard for her to see, so she grasped Rose's shoulder and let her lead the way. They weaved through the tree-shaped snow piles until her legs hurt. She was about to ask Rose to slow her pace when she suddenly stopped. Jen walked into her.

Rose turned to face her. She pulled Jen so close their cheeks were touching and pressed her lips against Jen's ear, saying in a low voice, "Wait here, Jen. I'll be right back."

Jen felt suddenly bereft as Rose disappeared into the swirling snowstorm. Boozer squirmed against her stomach, crying. Jen was filled with dread that Rose wouldn't come back at all. Just as the fear was beginning to take root, Rose reappeared and pulled Jen close again. "There are soldiers up ahead. They've built a small fire and look jumpy."

She guided Jen behind a thick copse of snow-shrouded trees. "Lie down here and wait. The trees will protect you from any stray bullets. I'll get you when it's safe."

Jen began to protest, but Rose had turned and vanished into the storm again. Jen felt useless, Boozer sticking his head out at her collar. She barely noticed the freezing snow as she held her breath and stayed as still as possible. She jumped when seven or eight gunshots rang out over the blizzard's wail.

Jen got up to a crouch. "Rose! Rose, are you okay?"

She waited for a response, but the wind was all she could hear. Boozer began to bark, a pitifully small noise against the blizzard's wail. His squirming became more frantic.

"Boozer, calm down," Jen implored. Boozer continued to fight her grip, finally getting loose from inside her coat and jumping into the snow.

"Boozer! You bad dog," Jen screamed as she climbed to her feet and followed the furrow in the snow that marked Boozer's passage.

Jen was having trouble staying on her feet, stumbling as the knee-high snow kept tripping her up. She was gripped by panic. "Boozer! Rose! Where are you, Rose?"

She thought she heard Boozer's yipping bark up ahead, but the gusting wind made determining the exact direction difficult. Jen nearly fell over as she stopped short at the scene before her. Six men in soldier's uniforms sat in a circle with Rose and Boozer. Rose's body was wreathed in pale blue fire while a flickering wall of identical flame circled their impromptu campsite. The ground within the wall of fire was dry and free of snow. The soldiers' own pitiful campfire was smoldering and forgotten. Rose noticed Jen and smiled. "Join us. It looks like we might have some allies who have a score to settle with Baba Yaga."

CHAPTER 32

Storm Front

M aster Kessler, the Keeper of Shadows, stood breathlessly within the snowless clearing, Yuri next to him. It was midnight, and the stars flickered in the circle of sky visible above the clearing. Before them was a spectral peasant's hut from a bygone era, lit by sputtering torches bracketing the door and a bonfire in the yard.

They entered the gate leading through the fence of bone and stood at the hut's threshold.

"We are here, greatest of all witches. I have come as you commanded," Kessler announced in a loud voice.

Despite the cold lump in his stomach, Yuri's lip curled in annoyance at his boss's subservient tone.

The door creaked open, and something stirred in the darkness within. Without warning, Baba Yaga's spindly form unfurled itself from the shadows, like a great bat venturing forth from its cave.

Yuri shuddered at the sight of the towering hag in tattered, innocuous peasant's garb. Her empty black eyes considered them both, and then she smiled, revealing her glinting iron fangs. She spoke in a whisper, an ancient proto-Russian difficult for Yuri to follow. Kessler listened intently, nodding when she'd finished.

He motioned toward the damaged Russian military vehicles at the edge of the clearing. "Yuri, gather any dead soldiers whose heads are still intact. They will bolster our numbers until Grandmother has fully manifested."

Yuri realized the witch was as ghostly as her hut, but even as she'd spoken, she'd gained some substance.

Yuri did as he was told, dragging forty-two corpses into the clearing halfway between the blizzard and the witch's hut.

Kessler stepped forward and raised his arms, calling out incantations until the dead bodies began to rise.

Kessler snapped at Yuri, "The talisman!"

Yuri reached into the canvas satchel he was wearing and pulled out the dusty skull. Kessler, followed by Yuri, walked back to Baba Yaga. Yuri held the skull out, and the witch reached with long, spindly fingers to touch it but stopped just short. She looked at Yuri and pointed to the part of the bone fence that was missing a skull.

Kessler turned to Yuri. "Get into position so we'll be ready when the time comes."

Both Yuri and the bound Grendel felt a surge of anger at the order but swallowed their rising rage. Yuri went to the fence, the grim smile on his lips unseen by Kessler or the ancient witch. It wouldn't be over until it was over.

*****

The oversized military transport plowed through the snowstorm as Francis, Ramos, and Alex tried to get warm stuffed in the heated cab with the driver.

"Thank you. We would have died out there if not for your help, Mr. ..." Francis glanced at the older, impeccably dressed man of Middle Eastern ancestry.

"Hamad. You may call me Mr. Hamad," he offered graciously. No one noticed Alex's troubled expression.

When Ramos could feel his hands again, he turned to Hamad. "Your English is perfect. Are you from around here?"

Hamad smiled but continued to look at the road ahead. "Oh no. Business brings me here. It should be done with soon though."

Alex blurted out, "The Pharaoh Club! You were the one who Rose went to talk to at the Pharaoh Club!"

Hamad showed no reaction to Alex's outburst.

Francis watched Hamad as he asked Alex, "Do you know him? What's the Pharaoh Club?"

Before Alex could answer, Hamad said, sounding sad though his expression didn't change, "You mean you didn't share your adventure with your father or the police detective here? I really must do something to make my club more memorable."

Francis realized that this ride wasn't what it appeared. "What do you want? Why did you pick us up?"

Hamad shrugged. "I thought that at least Alex would like to see the final act. We should be arriving at the clearing soon. You will get to see all my planning come to fruition."

A dawning sense of comprehension transformed Alex's face. "What do you mean?"

Hamad still kept his eyes on the road. "I suppose it started with Kessler, the Keeper of Shadows, one of the two remaining Atlani. He took one too many expeditions into other dimensions. He returned with the creature he calls Kibit, and his dedication to keeping the Twilight Veil strong and secure began to falter. Recognizing his negligence, my plan began to take form. The only thing that could derail it was the Archivist, the one you call Rose."

Ramos shook his head in disgust. "*Mierda!* It was you all this time? You're the reason for this fucking nightmare?"

Hamad seemed pleased with himself. "The Archivist and I have had an understanding for quite some time. I would leave her and her fellow Atlani to their duties, unmolested. In return, I would be given a remote and hidden lair located at the junction of a number of ley lines so I could sate my hunger and leave humanity to their own petty devices. Building the club was my idea, to help supplement my diet with the residual magical energy from the amateur workers of the Art.

"Then the flow of magic began to weaken, barely sustaining me. The Archivist's greatest fault was she remained a general until the end, putting far too much faith in honor, oaths, and mutual agreements. Rendering the Archivist helpless was simple when I invited her to the club. I handed her over to Kessler's thugs, and they shot her. I returned after they'd left her broken body behind and placed the enchanted dragon's tooth in her wound to remove her identity and cripple her ability to interfere in my plans. If she couldn't remember our agreement, she was in no position to enforce it.

"Manipulating and guiding Kessler was child's play. Now it is time to reap the rewards of my efforts before sending Baba Yaga back to the spirit realm she came from."

Alex looked like he was going to be ill. "Why would you do that? Why would you hurt Rose?"

Lust suddenly laced Hamad's voice. "As I said, the flow of magic in this world can no longer satisfy me. By breaching the Twilight Veil, I shall be able to feed again until I am sated. As for the Archivist, she employs items crafted from the bones of my ancestors. I cannot let such an affront stand without punishment."

Hamad turned his gaze on his passengers. Francis felt a crushing mental weight that made coherent thought or movement impossible. Francis could hear Alex and Ramos struggling as well.

Hamad's eyes had become something other than human. "It will all be over soon."

CHAPTER 33

Baba Yaga

Rose reached the edge of the blizzard and inspected the dark clearing where the snow didn't fall. The light from a bonfire within the bone fence threw diminishing illumination out to the edges of the snow-free zone.

Next to the hut stood Baba Yaga, like some sort of living scarecrow. Kessler stood facing her while Yuri stood near the fence of human bone surrounding the hut, a skull in his hand. Rose could sense the tear in the Twilight Veil several feet above the hut's roof, raw energy rushing through, powering the storm, throwing the mystical plane into chaos. Only the aura surrounding Baba Yaga was stronger, a terrible, malignant clot of magical energy that made Rose nauseous. Dead Russian soldiers shambled around the perimeter of the clearing in the dim, flickering light, no doubt bound to spirits that Kessler had called up.

Jen was crouched behind Rose holding Boozer, while Colonel Popov and his remaining Spetsnaz soldiers had taken a position near the wrecked military vehicles a hundred meters to Rose's left, taking advantage of the shadowy tree line. Popov was a military officer, so she left him to decide how to proceed with his men. Her only advice to them was to aim for the heads of their fallen comrades.

Rose now hesitated, at a loss as to what to do. The skull was the anchor keeping the witch here. Getting the skull would seem the first order of business. A plan took shape. If she could get the Russian soldiers to fire at Yuri, it might draw him and the Grendel away from the fence. If he didn't fall for the ruse, she could engage him, distract him while ... what? Jen snatched the skull? Rose's determination to keep her friends out of this had already failed miserably, and yet she still hesitated.

Jen pulled on her sleeve. "What are we going to do, Rose?"

"Stay with me, whatever happens," she called back to Jen. Rose took a deep breath and got ready to move when someone new walked into the clearing; despite the shadowy light at the edge of the clearing, she could see it was Hamad from the Pharaoh Club. She also saw Francis, Alex, and Ramos emerge from the blizzard just behind him, looking cold, unsteady, and miserable.

*****

Hamad took in the scene as he walked calmly toward the witch's hut. The Keeper of Shadows had bound spirits into the bodies of dead soldiers, a trio of which rushed forward to stop him. Hamad swatted them away like the gnats they were. He could already feel the flow of mystical energy crackling around him. The tear in the Veil was clear to him, and he could see it was still possible to repair. Once he was done feeding, of course.

*****

Kessler was filled with rage and fear as Hamad approached. The spirit bound within him took advantage of his sudden lack of focus, filling him with bloodlust and nightmarish visions. He closed his eyes and fought to regain control from the parasitic entity inside him, thankful he had fed it before coming here. It fought against him but could not prevail, finally being pushed back into the recesses of his mind.

Kessler took a breath and then left Baba Yaga to intercept Hamad, gesturing to the remaining dead soldiers to stop their assault. The Keeper of Shadows stopped several paces from Hamad, his usually calm voice cracking with annoyance. "What is your game, Hamad? It is far too late to stop this."

Hamad halted as well. "Ah, Keeper of Shadows. How wretchedly you have failed in your duties to your people. It would appear the Atlani's exile is a permanent one."

At this point Kibit leapt from the shadows onto Kessler's shoulder, its glowing red eyes fixed on Hamad.

Hamad smiled. "Ah, the architect of your plan makes an appearance. Do you realize how much you owe to your pet? You have done its bidding like a loyal slave."

Kessler was taken aback. "You lie, Hamad! This was my plan all along." But Kessler felt doubt creep into his mind. He remembered first finding Kibit decades before while exploring a gloomy, forested dimension. There had been an immediate connection, a mystic link that many practitioners of the Art described when finding a familiar. Kibit was no more than that.

The Keeper of Shadows let the blood spirit rise, let its madness devour Hamad's words. He prepared to feed the spirit dwelling in him.

"Enough of this, Hamad," Kessler hissed, raising his shades and looking into Hamad's eyes.

Hamad flinched and then slowly smiled, returning Kessler's gaze. Kessler had never been resisted before. What had happened to Hamad's eyes? They were now reptilian and … ageless. The Keeper of Shadows focused the entirety of his iron will and drew on his millennia of experience, locking himself in a test of wills with Hamad. For a moment, they seemed evenly matched. Then Kessler broke, a torrent of images smashing into the Keeper of Shadow's mind. He finally realized what Hamad was and began to scream, clawing at his eyes as if he could tear away the staggering revelation. He fell to the ground, gibbering and screaming as his shattered mind collapsed upon itself.

*****

Yuri watched the scene unfold and couldn't help feel pleasure as Kessler fell shrieking to the ground. He watched Kibit jump away, running back to Baba Yaga and leaping into her ghostly arms. She stroked the creature as if it were her beloved pet. Yuri guessed it was.

Then the Grendel took control of Yuri. The skull he'd been holding fell to the ground as his body painfully twisted and grew. His mind was locked away as the enormous brute roared and charged toward Hamad. It built up speed, its fang-filled maw slavering with murderous hunger. Then it caught the Archivist's scent and saw her watching from the darkness of the tree line. For a moment, the beast was torn between two equally urgent targets, and its pace slackened. After hesitating, it decided to strike the closer target and leapt toward Hamad.

Deep in the Grendel's mind, Yuri felt disquiet at how Hamad just waited for the attack with no hint of fear. As the Grendel reached him, Hamad grabbed the Grendel's shaggy mane, stopping the monster's momentum, and then slammed its head into the ground. As the Grendel lay there stunned, trying to recover its senses, Hamad curled his hands into fists and brought both down on the Grendel's head. With the sound of crunching bone, blood sprayed from the monster's nose, eyes, and ears. Yuri fell into blackness.

*****

Rose was dumbfounded. What in the name of the Goddess had just happened? Hamad brushed off his suit before continuing toward the witch. Then Rose noticed Francis, clutching a Russian assault rifle, running in the direction of the dropped skull. Alex and Ramos were following, trying to keep up. She sprinted into the clearing, drawing her sword from her duster. Jen stayed right behind her.

By now Hamad had stepped up to the bone gate that led to Baba Yaga and her hut. "Your time here is over, Witch. Return to the realm of spirits, and allow me to feed before the way is closed again."

The witch's cackle was mocking. Rose could just make out Baba Yaga's words, ancient as the dialect was. "Ignorant, bloated pig. You have been absent too long, have become weak like all the inhabitants of this *physical* realm."

Hamad's smug smile faded, and a look of anger replaced it. "I would have never imagined you were such a fool, Witch! Now it is time to learn your place in the scheme of things."

A shockwave erupted from Hamad, the ground rippling and breaking. Rose was knocked off her feet along with everyone else in the clearing. Only Baba Yaga remained standing.

The ground continued shaking as Hamad swelled into his true form: a towering, metallic-scaled behemoth with vast leathern wings and a lashing tail covered with bone spikes. The dragon reared back as it drew in air, then exhaled a torrent of flame upon the witch.

Rose jumped on top of Jen to shield her from the blistering wave of heat. Jen let out a muffled scream, and Boozer let out a yip.

Rose's leather duster had shielded them from the worst of it, but her fur-lined jacket was ruined, and her hair was singed and smoking. Hamad was the Ancient from her dream. Why was he here?

Francis continued crawling after being knocked over as Hamad had changed. He reached the fence and scooped up the skull. He knew he'd suffered second-degree burns on his face and arms from the dragon's fire. He managed to catch Rose's eye and hold up the skull triumphantly. He was too far away to throw it to her but managed to get to his feet and call out, "Alex, catch."

He tossed the skull as Alex fought to get to his feet. Francis felt a stab of pride as his son caught the skull. He watched Alex sprint across the clearing, trying to get nearer to Rose. Francis leveled his rifle and began spraying bullets at the dead soldiers, the witch, and the dragon, hoping to buy his son some time. Detective Ramos had grabbed a rifle as well and was sniping at the converging mass of undead Russian soldiers.

An unscathed Baba Yaga turned to Kibit, muttering darkly to the small creature.

Rose grabbed Jen, pulled her to her feet, and barely dodged Hamad's lashing tail. Boozer was loose, running as fast as his gimpy gait would carry him to Alex.

Kibit leapt from the witch's arms and ran to intercept Alex. One second, he was a scurrying, weasel-like animal and the next, the gaunt boy who had stolen the skull from the Dancing Hut. He held a long knife in one hand.

Alex watched the creature's approach, filled not with fear but anger. He waited until the child leapt at him before he threw the skull to Ramos, adrenaline and testosterone causing his heart to race. Alex was knocked to the ground, but the thing on top of him was interested only in the skull. It immediately tensed to give chase when Alex grabbed the child and rolled on top of him, pinning him on the hard dirt. Alex grabbed his hair and began slamming the demon-child's head into the ground.

At first the child simply struggled to escape Alex. Then Alex heard a hiss of anger, and with unexpected strength, the child twisted and slammed Alex onto his back, straddling him. Alex began to punch the sickly boy in the face, feeling nothing but an all-consuming rage. The child was caught off guard but then began bringing the knife down repeatedly, stabbing Alex again and again. Alex barely noticed the pain as he continued striking out at the thing on top of him. Finally his arms wouldn't respond anymore, and he began to get very dizzy. At some point the sickly child left him.

Alex knew he was fading, gripped by severe shock just like he'd been in the accident that had killed his mother. A spreading cold and a knot of nausea dulled all his other senses. At the moment, death didn't seem so bad. In fact, he looked forward to it. No more shame, self-loathing, sadness, or anger. He was weary of trying to fit into a world he didn't belong. If there was an afterlife, he had a long list of questions for whoever was in charge, and if there was nothing beyond death, he looked forward to the restful oblivion. As everything around him faded to black, he smiled.

Rose crouched, shielding Jen as gunfire broke out. Popov and his soldiers entered the clearing and began firing their AK-97s at their former comrades and the dragon.

Hamad hissed and bared his teeth as he saw Baba Yaga was untouched by his dragonfire. Rose shielded her eyes and turned away as the witch began drawing power directly from the tear in the veil, her foul aura now overwhelming in its radiance.

Hamad roared, his lashing tail smashing two of the dead soldiers who had wandered too close. Baba Yaga wove a mesh of magical energy around the dragon and lifted him off the ground. The air quaked as Hamad bellowed his outrage, struggling to break free of the witch's mystical web.

"Return home, fool, and remember your true self," she muttered just loud enough for Rose to hear; then, with a wave of her hand, the dragon was hurled through the tear in the Twilight Veil, disappearing into whatever formless dimension lay beyond.

"Do not think I have forgotten you, Keeper of Shadows. You may join Hamad in the release I promised you." She wove a single strand of mystical energy, twisted it around a sobbing Kessler, and hurled him through the tear as well.

Rose realized time was running out. The witch and her hut were nearly solid. The battle raged around the clearing as Popov and his men continued fighting the dead soldiers. Alex was down, and Ramos was on the ground wrestling with the demon-child, his rifle and the skull on the ground nearby. With one hand he was trying to hold the child's bloody knife at bay while he fumbled for his pistol with the other. The child switched the knife to his other hand and slashed Ramos's throat just as Ramos pushed his pistol up against the child's chest and fired. Ramos clutched his bleeding neck as the child fell backward off him and shifted back into an ember-eyed animal. Ramos continued to hold his throat as Kibit thrashed around on the ground until it grew still and dissolved into black smoke.

Boozer grabbed the skull in his mouth and was now dragging it around the clearing, running from anyone or anything that got near.

Francis ran up to Rose and hugged her. She closed her eyes and returned the hug, trying to find courage and strength as her friends died around her.

Jen grabbed her arm. "The skull. What happens if you throw the skull where the dragon and Kessler disappeared?"

Rose let Jen's words sink in, feeling like an idiot for not seeing it sooner. She pulled two silver throwing blades from her duster and gave one to Jen and one to Francis. "I'll keep the witch occupied. Get the skull, and throw it into the spot just above the witch's hut. These weapons should hurt anyone who gets in your way."

Without looking back, Rose ran toward Baba Yaga, sword in hand, and prayed to the Goddess that she wasn't too late.

CHAPTER 34

The Twilight Veil

The ancient witch was waiting as Rose passed through the gate of human bones and stopped within a few feet of her.

Rose did her best to sound respectful but kept the sword at her side. "Grandmother, this needs to end. This world and its people must walk their own road, make their own mistakes, learn and move forward at their own pace."

Baba Yaga cocked her head, her black eyes unreadable. "Why do you oppose me, Archivist? You of all should understand the need to punish this world. Injustice, cruelty, and selfish evil must be met with the same. *That* is how they will learn."

Rose's eyes widened as something passed through the tear in the Twilight Veil, something with a powerful aura but without form. It disappeared into the blizzard. Another followed almost immediately.

The witch's fangs glinted as she smiled. "It would seem the skull was not necessary. I have grown strong enough to act as a beacon to my children. Now they will come."

Rose felt her blood run cold. "What do you mean, children?"

Baba Yaga motioned, and her antique hut rose, standing upon a pair of huge avian legs. "Dispose of any who might interfere," the witch commanded.

The hut strode forward, hopping over the fence, and set off into the nighttime clearing after the Russian soldiers who had almost finished laying their dead comrades to rest.

The witch turned her attention back to Rose. "I have taught others from beyond the Veil to create and maintain physical form in this world. They shall be the instruments of my wrath."

Even as she spoke, more of the formless beings passed through the dimensional tear.

Rose willed the energy to rise within her, pale blue fire bursting from her body and forming a fiery nimbus of armor around her. She charged at the witch, her sword whistling around her as she became a blur of motion, dancing in a complex attack pattern, looking for an opening. Each time she tried to drive her weapon home, Baba Yaga simply used her hand to block the sword with contemptuous ease.

"What an impressive weapon, Archivist. I'm sure Hamad held a grudge against you until the end. Dragon bone imbues weapons with such great power. Your people understood such things," Baba Yaga muttered in her archaic dialect, a note of sadness in her voice. Suddenly the witch lunged forward, her long, ragged fingernails tearing through Rose's pale blue nimbus and across her midsection, cutting deeply, exposing muscle and bone. Rose fell to her knees, fighting to keep her grip on the sword as she clutched her hemorrhaging stomach with her free hand and choked in pain.

The witch smiled down at her. "Now it ends, Archivist. You and your bound spirit will be cast beyond the Twilight Veil and be torn asunder. You will no longer stand as a defender of the worthless humans here."

Out of the corner of her eye, Rose saw Jen and Francis trying to move stealthily nearer. Rose lifted her sword slowly then thrust it through Baba Yaga's leg. The witch shrieked as the smell of burning flesh stung Rose's nostrils, the enchanted silver searing the witch with its touch. Baba Yaga struck Rose across the face and sent her rolling beyond the bone fence and into the clearing.

Rose's head was spinning, but she was dimly aware of Francis's silver throwing blade protruding from Baba Yaga's eye socket. Then a voice called out, "Time for you to go back to hell, you bitch!" It was Jen, holding Boozer under one arm and hurling the skull with the other.

Rose and Francis had succeeded in distracting the witch long enough to prevent her from stopping what was about to happen. Baba Yaga hissed and clenched her hand into a fist. The skeletal fence exploded sending sharp, finger-sized shards of bone shooting in all directions.

Rose suddenly lost sight of the scene as Francis threw himself on top of her, putting his body between her and the fence.

Even without seeing it, Rose could sense the skull sail through the tear in the Twilight Veil. In the blink of an eye Baba Yaga, her hut, her bone fence, and her foul perversions of the Art were drawn into the rift, leaving an empty clearing behind. The blizzard stopped, leaving only a night sky above as far as they could see. The horizon was being touched by the first blush of dawn. The Twilight Veil was sealed.

Francis slumped on top of her, his back pierced by a fatal number of the sharp slivers of bone. Tears filled Rose's eyes when she realized he was gone.

Jen was lying motionless on the ground nearby, a bleeding Boozer whimpering several feet away. Rose struggled out from under Francis and climbed to her feet, rushing over to kneel at Jen's side. Most of the bone shards had vanished with the witch, but those that had found their mark remained. Jen looked up at Rose, blood dripping from her mouth, shock making her gaze seem distant. "Did we do it? Is she gone?"

Rose choked back a sob, nodding to her friend.

Colonel Popov and his two surviving soldiers approached, keeping a respectful distance. Jen reached up and touched Rose's cheek. "Don't cry, Rose. Everything will be all right."

Rose could sense the flickering embers of those who clung to life and knew her healing couldn't help them. What of the entities that had made it through the rift, Baba Yaga's children? Had they been drawn back when the rift was closed, or did they remain?

She'd failed her friends, failed the only people who meant anything to her. She might have failed the world as well. Rose's fragile sense of control crumbled, and she broke down, sobbing in despair. Power erupted from some secret place deep inside her. She heard Ayesha's faint voice begging her to stop, warning her of the terrible danger. She didn't care. As the energy surged through her, she fought all her instincts to control, direct, or shape it. As her power reached its crescendo, she surrendered to it.

People as far away as Volgograd reported seeing blue fire crackle across the morning sky like the aurora borealis.

CHAPTER 35

Aftermath

J en awoke in a warm bed, feeling better than she should have. She winced as Boozer leapt up and licked her face. An annoyed nurse came over and lifted the small dog off the bed and set it on the tiled floor. Jen looked around at the hospital ward, seeing Detective Ramos in the bed next to her, sleeping. The nurse said something to her in Russian, but she could only shrug apologetically at the woman, not understanding.

The nurse left and returned a moment later with one of the Russian soldiers who'd been in the clearing and who'd also seen the witch.

His English was surprisingly good. "Hello, young lady. I'm Colonel Popov. After the … incident, we made sure you and your companions were brought back to Volgograd and the hospital. I'm going to modify my report so you and your friends are not mentioned. A plane is waiting that will start your journey back to the west. Otherwise, you may never escape the wheels of the inquisitive Russian bureaucracy. Your presence here will create more questions than I have answers."

Jen looked around again, trying to find Rose or Alex, but they were nowhere to be seen. "Thank you, Colonel. Where are the others?"

Popov's face darkened. "I'm sorry. They didn't make it. I will see personally to their burial."

Jen felt her heart sink at the news, suddenly wanting to see Rose or Alex one last time. "Can I see them?"

Popov shook his head. "No. This hospital doesn't have a morgue. The dead were shipped to a facility some distance from here. Your time is short if you want to slip away before the Moscow officials arrive. As soon as we get a gurney for your male companion, we'll be on our way to the airstrip. You're both healthy enough to travel."

Jen placed a hand over her ribs where she'd been pierced by several bone shards. Her skin was smooth, unscarred. There was no pain. Instead of relief, she felt a chill run up her spine. The chill remained with her all the way to the waiting airplane.

*****

The doctor's words kept repeating themselves in her head: *I'm sorry, Miss Sinclair, but the tests indicate that you're infertile."*

She hadn't had her period for two months, ever since returning from Russia. She'd had fears of some otherworldly pregnancy or something even worse, but infertile? She was only twenty-two. It was as if menopause had come and gone while she was sleeping. Jen was awash in conflicting emotions. She felt lost without Alex or Rose. She could have used their strength right now.

She pulled her rattling Toyota into the parking lot of a run-down liquor store she happened to notice. She didn't usually drink, but she needed something other than cola right now. She also needed to get some dog food for Boozer, who was now her responsibility since their landlady, Miss Shaw, had died of a heart attack while they were in Russia. Boozer was no longer gimpy, either, constantly running full speed around the apartment, usually in the middle of the night. Did liquor stores carry dog food? She'd never checked.

It was mid-afternoon, and the frontage road she'd been driving along had been empty. She got out of her car, the cold winter breeze bringing back painful memories—being in Russia, mortally hurt, and Rose's anguished face hanging above her, crying. Jen's heart broke whenever she remembered, as if all the sorrow of a lifetime had been distilled into a single moment, Rose trapped within it.

She stepped into the harsh florescent light of the store, and rows of alcoholic beverages beckoned her. She glanced around and realized the store was as empty as the street. Even the cashier wasn't at his post. She went to the rum section and perused the labels. She had enough cola at home for a week's worth of rum and Coke.

She tucked the bottle under her arm and fumbled for her billfold as she walked up to the counter, hoping there was a bell to ring to get service. When she looked up, a man was standing there, pointing a revolver at her. That's when she noticed the smell of cordite, just like in Russia, noticed the manic look in the gunman's eyes, and saw the figure on the floor behind the counter in a pool of blood.

As all this fell into place, she had the ridiculous thought that this couldn't happen to her. She'd helped save the world.

The man fired the revolver two times. It felt like she'd been shoved hard by someone as she fell backward and hit the floor. Then the pain came, like a terrible fire inside her chest. The gunman turned his attention to the cash register, hitting it with his gun again and again as he tried to open it. He ignored her as she died on the floor. It was the last thing she saw as blackness mercifully took her.

Jen screamed as she awoke. She was on an exam tale with medical personnel all around her, cutting off her blood soaked clothes and attaching wires to her with adhesive tabs. She began to cry as people talked all around her.

"We have a heartbeat doctor. Blood pressure it good."

"Where are the entry points? Can anyone see?"

"Nurse, she's waking up. Sedate her."

The fear and commotion faded as Jen slipped back into darkness.

Stephen Ramos was sitting next to Jen's hospital bed reading a magazine when she woke up.

He set the magazine aside gave her a weary smile. "Hello, Miss Sinclair. How are you feeling?"

She felt a stab of irritation, "Call me Jen or Jenna! Hell, Stephen, we were in a war together."

"I'm sorry, force of habit. Business first though. Could you give me a description of the gunman?"

She did her best to recall what the man was wearing, his hair, eyes, general appearance, telling Detective Ramos everything she could remember.

Once he was done taking her statement, he seemed to relax. "So how are you holding up, Jen?"

She made a poor effort at a laugh. "I'm still here, aren't I? That psychopath didn't even blink when he shot me. Twice."

Stephen leaned forward and spoke softly to her. "When the paramedics got to you, you had no pulse and weren't breathing. They worked on reviving you all the way to the hospital with no luck. Then in the emergency room you just woke up, your vitals all in the green, no gunshot wounds to be found, and two bullets tangled in your bloody clothes. The doctors are at a total loss."

Jen was quiet, not sure how to answer. She could see that Ramos was just as stumped as she was.

She bit her lower lip. "It's like I came back from the dead, just like Rose. What did she do to us in Russia?"

Ramos looked tired. "Guess we should expect strange things where Rose was involved. Ever since I first laid eyes on that woman, my life had become as convoluted as trying to solve a broken Rubik's Cube."

Jen thought about Ramos' words. "Stephen, have you been getting texts with weird characters and emojis?"

Ramos looked at her, eyes widening. "*Mierda!* Yeah, about once a week, ever since we got back from Russia. Tried to block them, but they just kept coming." He pulled out his phone and checked his messages, having received one just yesterday.

He cursed under his breath as recognition dawned. "Shit! These are the symbols that were etched on Rose's amulet. God, I'm an idiot! Look at the emojis—a red flower, a black bird, a cluster of trees, and a cross with a loop on top. I got the first three—Rose Ravenwood."

Jen added with excitement, "The last symbol … is an ankh. It was from ancient Egypt—the Pharaoh Club, of course! Does this mean Rose is still alive?"

Detective Ramos considered her question, wondering if it could be Reginald instead. He'd gone to Ravenwood Tower after they'd gotten back from Russia. The only person left was the doorman in the lobby. He'd told Ramos that the place had been vacated and that he had no forwarding address for Reginald or Miss Ravenwood. He was being paid to just watch the place and keep out troublemakers.

Ramos asked, "So where is this Pharaoh Club exactly?"

Jen closed her eyes and suddenly felt very tired. She managed a hopeful smile. "It's not far."

Then her expression became alarmed. "Oh God, I forgot about Boozer! Can you retrieve my apartment key and go feed him?! He needs to be taken out too so he can do his business too!"

Ramos looked at her askance. "Can't you call someone? In case you've forgotten, Boozer and I don't get along."

She grabbed his jacket sleeve and was surprised by the desperation in her voice. "Please Stephen. Just look after him until I get out of the hospital."

He sagged and nodded. "Just this once."

Jen squeezed his arm and sunk back onto the bed. "When I'm feeling better, the three of us can go to the club together. With Hamad gone, maybe they have new management."

EPILOGUE

The Cosmo club was busy tonight, the dance floor choked with gyrating, spinning revelers blowing off steam on a Friday night. The big man watched the scene from his shadowy booth, sitting alone. No one joined him. Something about him made people uneasy. His attention was focused on a striking blond woman in a black dress that showed off her breathtaking figure. He was sure it was Joanna Pryce. She was working the men at the bar, looking for the right victim to feed on. He enjoyed watching her hunt, admired her technique—how she drew them in with her overt sexuality combined with an innocent, girl-next-door prettiness.

She finally left with a businessman in a nice suit too drunk to walk straight, so she helpfully guided him outside. The big man left his booth, and the throng parted nervously for him as he followed her.

The businessman put up more of a fight than Joanna had expected; he must work out. The dark alley and location behind some dumpsters hid his desperate attempts to break her embrace. As soon as her fangs sank into his neck, his will to resist subsided and she greedily drank the blood gushing from his neck. It was only when his heart stopped that the blood ceased flowing. She let him sink to the ground as she felt his warm blood filling her and the hunger subside while the terrible guilt clenched her unbeating heart. She wiped the dark smears from her mouth with his jacket, then rifled through his pockets until she found his wallet. She took only the cash and tossed the wallet back into a trash can.

Joanna glanced down the alley, making sure no one was watching, and then lifted the hundred-and-eighty pound corpse effortlessly, tossing him in an open dumpster. She reached in and twisted his head off, wincing with disgust. She placed the severed head in a separate dumpster. She concealed both under as much trash as she could pile on them, leaving her victim for the garbage men to dispose of.

She turned to leave the alley and stopped. A large man was blocking her exit, watching her. He wore wrap-around shades despite it being night.

She crouched slightly, ready to attack the intruder.

He said with a Slavic accent, "Nurse Pryce, I've been looking for you."

Despite his immense size, her condition would allow her to easily knock him aside and flee. One second she was rushing him, the next he'd backhanded her half way back down the alley. She should have slammed into the ground but, due to her heightened reflexes, managed to land in a cat-like crouch. Her head was still ringing though.

He chuckled and advanced. "Zer's no need to be rude, Nurse Pryce. We are kindred spirits, you and I. Slaves to master that no longer exists."

She looked up at him and examined the stranger more closely. He did look familiar, and suddenly she remembered. "Oh God, you're the one from the hospital who turned into a monster. You were with the man who did this to me!"

He nodded. "You are fortunate. Kessler usually killed anyone he fed from. I think you just slipped his mind in all zee excitement. He's gone now and von't be coming back."

He removed his shades. His eyes were empty and leprous white. When he smiled, she shuddered; his mouth was unnaturally wide and filled with too many sharp teeth. "My 'monster' and I have come to arrangement. I am Yuri. Come, vee have much to discuss."

Joanna Pryce cautiously followed as Yuri turned and exited the alley.

Neither noticed the small, black furred creature with glowing red eyes watching them from the fire escape above.

AUTHOR DESCRIPTION

Michael S. Ripley was born in the Monterey Bay area of Central California, in an age before cell phones and home computers. His formative years were heavily influenced by dinosaurs, Ray Bradbury, Avalon Hill war games, J. R. R. Tolkien, Dungeons & Dragons, Godzilla, and H. P. Lovecraft. After graduating from high school, he spent four years in the US Army spying on the East Germans during the Cold War. After his military stint, he earned a four-year degree in European history, with a minor in military history, from San Jose State University and began working for the Santa Cruz Public Library. He's been there thirty years and counting. When not at work, he spends time with his partner Caroline or playing games with his current RPG group. This is his first book.

ABOUT THE BOOK

Silicon Valley is the birthplace of the high-tech, modern world. Even here, in this shining testament to the heights of human achievement, ancient forces hide in the shadows, pursuing their own agendas. A homicide investigation triggers a series of events that will cause the two worlds to collide. A woman awakes with no memory and tries to piece together her past, finding unexpected allies and sinister enemies along the way. Her personal quest becomes a race against time as a dark legend threatens to become all too real, leaving the fate of the world hanging in the balance.

CPSIA information can be obtained
at www.ICGtesting.com
Printed in the USA
LVHW111015081019
633401LV00010B/803/P